PRIZED

THE LEGION: SAVAGE LANDS SECTOR

EVA PRIEST

AN UNDEFEATED GLADIATOR FIGHTS THE BATTLE OF HIS LIFE IN ORDER TO SAVE HIS FATED MATE.

MELISANDE

I've never been lucky in love. Tired of the lonely nights and the creepy dudes, I test out a new dating app. Figures that the first attractive profile I see, I swipe right and get transported across the galaxy.

Now I'm forced to be an escort to strange alien creatures. I despair of finding my way back home until a warrior invades my dream and gives me a cherished weapon: hope.

LYOVA

My latest assignment should have been easy. Go undercover as myself, taking up my previous mantle as an undefeated gladiator in the arenas. That will lure my latest bounty to me easily enough.

Fate has other plans. I not only end up ensnaring a vicious warlord, but also my mate.

I never dreamed of ever finding my fate-mate, but now that I have, I will fight the greatest battle of my life to keep her.

Prized is a full-length, stand-alone sci-fi alien romance that is set in The Legion: Savage Lands Sector universe. This series is full of fated mates, instalove, happily-ever-afters, overprotective alien males (that look like aliens!), and the headstrong females that love them.

Each book stands alone, but here is a suggested Reading Order:

Hunted
   Scorched
   Prized
   Freed

"WE ARE LEGION, FOR WE ARE MANY."

THE SAVAGE LANDS SECTOR

The Rodinians have long been assigned to the Legion's Reaper units, patrolling the harshest sectors of the galaxy.

When we're on the hunt, there is nowhere in the galaxy you can hide from us. Try it. We dare you. You'll see that we are already in the shadows, waiting for you.

Dear Reader,

Each story in The Legion Universe stands alone; however, if you would like to get a feel for this world and characters, I recommend reading *Hunted*, my first story in this series.

The first part of *Hunted* was published in the *Stolen and Seduced* anthology; I have since received my rights back, and have published it on its own on Amazon.

If you choose to start The Legion Universe with this book, that's fine too!

. . .

HAPPY READING!

MUCH LOVE,

Eva Priest

Rough hands curled over my breasts from behind, squeezing the mounds before scorching a trail down the side of my body and resting possessively on my hips. He was here again. My dream champion.

None other would treat me this way. Like I was precious. Like I mattered.

His touch was addictive. Decadent. Though the last two nights had been barely-remembered dreams, I clung to them, as they gave me renewed hope despite my reality.

I pushed those real-life intrusions aside for now. They didn't belong in this sacred space. Here, now, I focused on pure sensation.

The smooth, cold feel of the wall in front of

me. His large body behind me, radiating heat and strength with every caress. His skin was like supple suede stretched over steel.

How he made me feel like a goddess, and I gloried under his attention. With him, I could forget myself. At least for a little while.

"Where are you, my sweet?" The hint of command in his voice made me tremble. He'd asked this question before, but I still didn't know the answer. I wanted to obey, but I couldn't. And I couldn't bring myself to lie.

"I don't know."

"Would you tell me if you did?"

"Yes," I gasped. Slick flowed from between my legs. I squeezed my thighs together, but there was no hiding from him. His dark laughter made my heart race as he dragged his large hands down my body to cup my sex.

He parted my pussy lips and teased along my seam with a feather-light touch. "That's my good girl. Tell me your name."

"Melisande," I hissed, drawing out my name as I fell further into bliss. I wanted to drive my hips forward, increase the pressure of his finger against my clit, but he gripped my hips still. He was in absolute control here.

He carried on his playful, conversational tone as if he wasn't skillfully destroying my body. "A beautiful name for a beautiful female. You know my name, don't you, kitten? You screamed it for me when I made you come." Yes, I knew it. It was branded into my very soul. "Lyova." I pressed myself against his palm. He responded by holding me still. Oh yes, he was in absolute control.

I swallowed a sob.

I'd been with other men before, but nothing like this. Never responded anywhere close to this. He was attentive and hot and knew his way around my body.

He pressed his massive length against my back, cupping my sex to keep my writhing body still. His fingers dipped into my wet heat, testing me, stretching me. I let my head fall back so that it rested against his shoulder.

"Brace yourself against the wall, my sweet girl. There you are. Just like that."

He lined up our bodies and pushed himself inside of me. He met resistance and gently thrust in and out, swirling his finger over my clit. "Take all of me, my beauty," he urged. "You can do it." He angled my hips and pulled my thighs apart just a little more. Finally, he bottomed out, his entire length pulsing inside of me.

A primal growl rocked through his chest, vibrations coursing between us. "So tight." He dragged his length in and out of me, keeping me still so he could control the pace.

It made no difference to me. I ceded myself over to him. Gave him total control in this manner. Trusting him to take care of me.

His rhythm grew wild, hips smacking against me, fingers marking me. "Lyova! I can't hold on."

He nipped at my neck, trailing his teeth over the smooth contours of my shoulders before biting down. "Let go, my beauty. I've got you."

And he did have me. Without breaking his rhythm, he spun me around, so that I wrapped my legs around his hips, the wall at my back. He kept me safe in the cradle of his arms, pinioning my arms above me as he drove into me harder and harder.

I gave in to the most decadent orgasm yet. I screamed for him, chanting his name until I no longer had words, no longer had a voice. He threw his head back and roared, the sound of it echoing into the farthest reaches of my heart and soul.

I willed myself to remember this dream. It

would need to keep me company for many months to come. The worship in his golden eyes. The line of his body, the taut muscles, the way he gripped me, but never hurt me with his claws. The way his tail wrapped around my waist. Every part of him possessive of me.

I awakened in my bed, still feeling his delicate touches like kisses whispering against my skin. The dream dissipated like a fog on a dewy day and I found myself gazing up at the illuminating blue lights casting their neon glow. I touched myself, still feeling his caresses on my body. Still yearning for more. I touched my clit, imagining my fingers were his.

And then the light above me blinked, the bulb zeroing in on me.

I quickly pulled my hands away from myself, my libido dying.

I sighed as I slowly rose, pushing back the red tendrils framing my face. The glow of the clock on the nightstand showed that it was a couple hours before dawn. I still had some time to sleep. I probably should get some more rest.

Instead I rubbed the sleep from my eyes and turned my attention to the windows surrounding me, offering me a glorious view of the luxurious confines of my accommodations. Though I knew this building was filled with others like me, I rarely see more than passing shadows and silhouettes of who my neighbors were.

Just as well. I was moved around so often, it wasn't like I could make friends with anyone. That was the point, of course.

At least the sameness of each new apartment brought some level of comfort. I was always housed in an elite compound for female professional companions, or khosas, as they were called in Varon society. They were beautiful birds living in gilded cages.

Though I lived among them, I was not one of them. For one thing, I did not choose this life.

I was beamed here after trying out a new dating app.

A fucking dating app.

My friends had recommended them to me, telling me it had helped them meet what's-his-face who proposed last week, or that the men on the apps were actually interested in settling down.

Even if it had worked out for others, I always thought I would meet my soulmate in person. I would stumble upon him at some social event. He would lock eyes with me, smile, and eventually find his way over to me. We would fall in love, get married, and live happily ever after.

Instead, after a few glasses of wine and feeling particularly lonely one night, I finished filling out my profile on my umpteenth dating app and a few swipes later, I was beamed away and ended up with Isaul.

The mating cuffs that ensured my obedience were on my wrists before I even woke up.

The end. My happily never after.

"Lights," I called to the room around me, the soft blue turning into a bright golden glow.

I lived on the outer walls of the facility near the peak of the tall skyscraper. My rooms nestled in vast clouds spread out and golden as if I was in the heavens. It was a glorious treat.

"Do well and all you will ever know would be luxury," Isaul had whispered against my ear. I shivered, rubbing the goosebumps appearing at the sound of his voice. "Fail, and I will send you below the clouds to rot."

The clouds were the fine line separating the masses from the wealthy. I lived somewhere in the Concord of the Sovereign Worlds, yet Isaul moved me around so frequently I never knew exactly where I was. It didn't help that each facility was the same. Or even if I had that spectacular view, I would still see the same beautiful clouds and towering skyscrapers.

Below the clouds was the city life, filled with aircrafts flying from platform to platform. It wasn't beautiful, but at least it got some light. Unlike the streets far below where the undesirables lived off scraps, fighting and trying to claw their way out.

I'd been sent there once as punishment for refusing a job. One of my firsts. It had only taken me an hour before I was crying and begging for Isaul to take me back.

"It's all right, love," he'd whispered to me, petting my red hair. "I forgive you."

I shuddered, willing the memory away, yet I still heard the echoes of Isaul's voice. "You're lucky," he had said. "I rarely forgive. But you're special to me, Melisande."

There was no use looking back. This was my life now, and I had to make the most of it.

I grabbed the black robe hanging near my bedside and shoved my feet into the fluffy slippers before traipsing toward my vanity. The blue light hovering above followed me. It always followed me when I was having my break away from my duties. It watched my every move, whether waking or sleeping. As if it were Isaul himself hovering above me, gazing down at me.

I sat on a cushioned chair in front of my vanity. The lights surrounding the mirror beamed on with my presence. My reflection horrified me. My green eyes were rimmed red and framed with purple circles.

I looked like shit. Being paid to party and entertain took its toll on my skin. The Varons must have some hardy genetics to keep up with this kind of pace. But as a human, I needed more than just my "beauty sleep."

I could sleep a decade and I would still resemble a corpse with this lifestyle.

Pushing a button on the vanity, the console shifted to reveal a trifold mirror. A pleasant melody played, a cue for me to close my eyes while rejuvenating lights shone on me. After a series of beeps, the mirror retracted and the light dimmed. I looked rested and refreshed. The blue-violet glow revived the youthful glow and texture to my skin in seconds.

I took the brush and ran it through my hair. The action triggered a memory of Isaul sniffing it, bringing the strands to his lips before kissing them.

"Your hair is magnificent," I remembered him whispering as he watched me in the mirror.

I shuddered and ripped the brush through my fiery strands, hating every bit of it. I just had to be born with blood-red hair. But it wasn't just that. My hair had a natural ombre to it, where it lightened at the bottom. It was a mark of status here.

I ripped the brush through my locks again, my scalp burning from the ferocity.

"Melisande," I heard my name over comms.

I sighed and set down the brush.

What now?

"Yes," I called dutifully, resting my hands in my lap.

"Isaul is sending transport. You have an hour."

I quickly dabbed on some make-up accenting my eyes in brown eyeshadow and giving myself sultry red lips. Pinning my hair up, I left a few tendrils loose to frame my face. I shifted out of my robe, dropping it in a pile on the floor, followed by my pajamas. The light hovered around me, it's blinking bulb looking up and down my naked body, approaching my breasts, circling around to get an angle of my ass.

I rolled my eyes. It was obviously either Isaul hoping to get some videos for future clients, or a paying asshole jacking off on the other end. Most likely it was both.

Maybe they thought I was here because I enjoyed this kind of work. Some females did, and all the power to them, but me?

I pulled up the black straps of my maxi dress. It had slits going all the way up on either side yet covered my front and ass. It was sexy and comfortable. It was also Isaul's favorite.

The platform appeared and the window opened. I stuffed my feet into some highly uncomfortable stilettos before running out to meet my transport. Knowing me, I probably forgot something, but being late wasn't an option.

Isaul hated it when I was late.

And since my little mishap on the streets, I made sure I would never make Isaul angry ever again.

I was his broken-in perfect little pet, and what I hated most was that he knew it. He knew I would never go against him ever again.

I couldn't.

The straps circled around my legs and arms, holding me still as it left my room and lowered into the darkness of the facility below. I ignored the lurching in my stomach and closed my eyes, the wind within the skyscraper whipping at my face.

This part sucked. It was like I was on a roller-coaster ride without a bar to hold on to. I wished I could scream.

I frequently wished I could scream.

I opened one eye and sighed in relief when I saw Isaul's grey form awaiting below. He smirked as he watched me. His golden eyes scrutinizing my attire. He was dressed in a black cloak, the hood up, covering his balding head. White hairs poked out from beneath the hood.

Isaul stood surrounded by his guards, who ogled me discreetly as the platform lowered. I must be going somewhere extravagant, I thought as I saw the light-wing aircraft behind them and the gold and red attire his guards adorned.

The platform locked in place, my straps circling back into their slots. I lowered my hands to my side and slightly bowed my head. "Master Isaul," I whispered.

"Melisande," he stepped toward me, towering above me. I flinched when his fingers gripped my hair, thinking for a moment he would yank me by my strands. Instead he kissed the locks before stroking the side of his cheek with them. "Beautiful as always."

I didn't say anything. I didn't want to. I didn't want him to find me beautiful. I didn't want him touching me. Everything he did, I hated, and I wished there was more I could do to show my hatred for him.

But he was stronger. There was no way I could fight him.

In the end, it was just better to say nothing.

"You were glorious," he said, continuing to stroke my cheek as he circled me. His finger ran down the length of my exposed back. "I knew you werc the one for the job. Lord Ladonian paid a lot of money." He chuckled.

Lord Ladonian was my client last night and also a high ranking Varon in the Sovereign Worlds, who loved to wear white. White everything. White shoes. White suits. White hats. When we met, he was in an all-white suit and a white cravat which he spilled red wine all over when I slid my hand down his pants.

He was also a very big man with nearly nothing swinging between his legs.

Though that was tragic in and of itself, the lord's greatest fault was that he liked to talk. Isaul knew it, too, which is why he set up the job. It was almost too easy to draw his secrets out for Isaul's surveillance tech to record.

That was Isaul's secret, and why he was one of the most powerful Varons in the Sovereign Worlds. Sure, Isaul made plenty of money from his harem, but blackmail was where he truly made his millions. He had dirt on many higher-ups in the Sovereign Worlds. He had dirt on everyone. And, since he had acquired me, his earnings have skyrocketed.

"I sent the funds to your account, my precious." Isaul pet my shoulder as he pulled out the tablet that would show my earnings.

I closed my eyes, knowing what would happen next. I hated seeing the numbers, seeing how far away I was from my goal.

Isaul knew it too. He enjoyed taunting me like this.

"Alas, you still are far away from paying out your bonds."

I opened my eyes and saw the numbers. 13,500/5,133,900 it read; displaying the 13,500 in yellow and the 5,133,900 in red.

My debt.

The only way I could be free from Isaul was to

out-earn the massive lifestyle he had set up for me. Until then, I was his legally bound mate; his pretty bird that he kept in a beautiful prison.

If I was crazy enough, I would laugh.

"I do have another job for you," said Isaul, circling around to face me.

My eyes met his for a moment. He raised an eyebrow at my expression, and I quickly lowered my gaze down to the platform. Isaul held out a chip in front of my view, displaying the picture of the angriest looking Varon I had ever seen.

The male was tall and bulky. He had pink scars across his gray face and short orange hair cropped close to his skull. Yellow eyes stared back at me. It was as if he sneered at the photographer right before he broke the photographer's neck.

I swallowed my disgust.

"You could refuse," said Isaul. He sighed and rubbed his chin thoughtfully. "However, I don't think we can afford your place here if that is the case. Or your clothes for that matter. I would have to let you go, Melisande. You understand?"

Instead of answering, I took the chip from Isaul's hand, reading the name next to the picture.

Chorwan Vortu.

I can do this. I can do anything for a day or two.

Isaul snapped his fingers and the guards proceeded to the aircraft. I followed behind him, pocketing the chip.

"When do we begin?"

Isaul wrapped his arm around my shoulders and pulled me toward him. His lips lightly touched my ear. "Tonight."

I woke gasping for breath, hot cum and sweat coating my belly. My blankets were long discarded, thrown from me as if I'd been through a battle.

What the hell was that?

I used the twisted sheets to wipe the spent seed from my stomach. I'd never made this much of a nighttime mess, not even as a burgeoning youth. And yet, the intensity of the dream still clung to me, sucking me back into that unity bond. My cock hardened once more, standing proud against my abdomen. I wrapped my fist around it, imagining my mate's hot, wet pussy pulsing around me, milking me for all I had.

One stroke, two, and fuck, I was done.

That was no ordinary wet dream. No, that slice of perfection that had me believing in the old gods had been my fate-mate, and what we shared was the start of the unity bond. It would be stupid to deny it.

My raging hard-on was ample proof. Fuck, I needed to find her. Soon. My body wouldn't relent until I claimed her.

I wiped myself clean yet again, and stalked toward the lav. Her scent, though faint, teased my senses. I couldn't quite pin it down, and it killed me. I had felt everything else in the dream so intensely.

Three nights. This was the third night I'd dreamed of her, the first night that I remembered more than just her name. And what a night.

She already marked my heart and soul. Soon, she will leave her mark on my body when she bonds with me. And she would bond. There would be no doubt about that.

I faced the shower head, tapped the water pressure on high, and allowed the hot jets to blast against me. I welcomed the stinging heat and pain, but it did nothing to distract me from my mate.

Fisting my cock once more, I rubbed the sensitive underside, dragging my fingers over the ridges there. Imagined my mate cry out as I dragged my length in and out of her. Though my rough breathing echoed in the shower, it was my mate's sweet gasps that I heard as I re-played her pleasure. I stroked myself faster and faster, growling low in my throat as I spilled once more.

If I could come so much with just the idea of her, what in star's blazes would it feel like to be with her?

The unity dream was so intense this time, she had to be near. As in, the same city, and there was no telling if she would stay for long. She couldn't tell me where she was, and I hated to dwell upon the reason for her ignorance.

No matter. I was a Rodinian male serving as a Reaper for the Legion. And she was my fate-mate. I would find her. The question was: Would I be able to find her and secure her safely before I got in too deep with our cloaked op?

What if my quarry took me on a different path, one that diverged from my mate? There would be no question which path I would take, and none of the other Reapers would fault me for it.

Hell, they would have my back as I ran after her. Fate-mates were sacred.

I signaled a comm to my squad commander,

Cade Lonza. As Reaper One, he had found his fate-mate under duress during an assignment. He would know how I felt and would need to know how to coordinate the rest of the squad in case something happened.

I noticed the time. Two hours before dawn. I hesitated for just a moment before sending the comm, telling myself that he'd prefer to know now, even if he would also want to kill me.

I programmed the automator to make some darjara, a tea closest to the kava drink the human mates preferred. I took a long swallow as I watched dawn approach over the city, the red light piercing the shadows.

"Lyova," I heard Cade over comms. He spat my name as if he was cursing over every syllable. "This better be important."

I sighed as I tried to think of a good place to start. Maybe from the beginning? "Sorry, Cade, but I just woke up in my own jizz."

I heard a groan. "Lyova," Cade said, disgust dripping from each word, "I didn't need to know that."

I grimaced. That was probably the wrong place to start.

"If that was all you woke me up for, I swear on all the ancient gods--"

I shook my head. "Wait! Wait!" I heard rustling over comms and spoke quickly. "I started wrong. I'm all messed up. Forget what I said." I sighed, dropping my head into my hands. "I had a unity dream."

There was a brief pause. "Oh."

"I think my fate-mate is near." I ran a hand through my mane, setting down my darjara.

"What do you mean by near, Ly?"

"Near, as in this city near."

I heard a sigh. "That might be a problem."

I flopped down onto the sofa. "I know." I leaned back against the cushions, gazing up at the ceiling and imagining her face, her fiery red hair, those beautiful green eyes. "I need to find her, Cade. Which is why I contacted you. I don't want to jeopardize the mission, but I gotta find her."

I thought of Talus and how he met Callie while gathering intel on the Tane syndicate. He snatched her right in the middle of a deal, and there was barely any time for him to run. Star's blazes, Callie didn't even have translators. It was a damned miracle he got them both out of Erebus with barely a scratch.

Cade was most likely thinking the same and I could almost hear his mind grinding through the probabilities over the long pause on comms.

"I'll send you Dorn. Talus is away with Callie on their honeymoon."

I didn't like thinking of Cade and Solana without back-up of their own. Sure, they were a team to be reckoned with, and Cade could more than handle himself. I still felt uneasy. "What about you two? Will you be all right on your own? If you're called away, Solana would be unprotected."

"We'll possibly have new recruits. Legion command contacted me a few hours ago. Seems they were of the same mind as you and want more Reaper units housed on the Aurum."

The Aurum was Cade's warship, and our home base in the Savage Lands. Now that I knew Cade would have help, my worry lessened. "New recruits?" I smiled as I thought of my younger years as a new recruit. How reckless I once was... well, I guess that didn't really change. "Are you on babysitting duty?"

Cade scoffed. "It's not babysitting duty. New recruits means new recruits!"

I laughed, spinning my empty cup around in my hand. "Sure."

"We'll be fine here. Find your mate. Get the job done. I trust you can balance what needs to happen when the time comes. Just promise me one thing?"

I stopped my fidgeting. "What is that?"

"Never, ever awaken me in the middle of the night and begin with 'I woke up in my own jizz.'"

I barked in laughter. "You got it."

"Dorn will be contacting you soon. I'm going back to bed. Maybe you should too, oh great, magnificent, undefeated gladiator Lyova Artox."

I laughed. "You mean the most amazing, magnificent gladiator Lyova Artox who is not only undefeated, but has won sexiest gladiator of the year."

Cade groaned. "Don't let this go to your head."

I couldn't prevent the wicked smirk even if I tried. "Too late."

Another groan. "Good night."

"Good morning," I corrected. Cade didn't bother responding.

I sighed after comms ended, grabbing a refill of darjara from the automator, and taking a thoughtful sip. I moved near the window, watching the gold and crimson rays glimmer and light the skyscrapers surrounding me. The clouds hovered above, becoming more golden as the sun rose.

I peered below, seeing more neon. The skyscrapers continued down into the darkness. I barely made out the streets of the city planet, still dark from lack of light.

Already, light-wings zipped past. Screens hovered by my rooms, displaying advertisements for the day's tournament, flickering photographs of the opponents for today's challenges. I saw my image and imagined someone else staring out the window and seeing it as well.

Melisande.

Her name sent trickles down my spine. She was here in the Sovereign Worlds, most likely on this city planet.

Lyova. I shuddered as I remembered the sound of her voice.

But why was she here?

Worry trickled in as I remembered she didn't know where she was. I told myself not to worry about this ignorance, but now, being alone in my thoughts, I knew it wasn't good. Someone had her contained somewhere. The city was vast. Finding her was going to be difficult, especially if she was hidden somewhere. Maybe she couldn't even see these advertisements, otherwise she would know me. She would know I was here.

I rubbed my forehead, imagining her under me and I released a moan. It was as if she were here, touching me, calling for me. She was the most beautiful woman I had ever seen. I could cream myself just thinking about her eyes, how full of wanton pleasure they were as I thrust deep inside her.

But why was a human woman here of all places?

I took a shuddering breath and shook my head. If I continued thinking about her, I would be jacking myself the whole day.

The mission. Think about the mission, Ly.

I strode over toward the counter, grabbing the chip detailing my next bounty.

Chorwan Vortu, escaped warlord.

Star's blazes, was he ugly. I grimaced staring down at his scarred face and his giant veiny neck. I would not want to be in a room alone with him.

The mission was simple enough. Chorwan favored the arena and the gladiator tournaments. Made sense since he was a violent motherfucker who had cut off the face of his prison guard and worn it as a mask when he televised his escape.

A very sick motherfucker, I wanted to add, but here on Varonis Prime, he was pretty much untouchable. Especially during a tournament that was supposed to be like a peace treaty between the Sovereign Worlds and the Legion.

I pursed my lips just thinking of that whole fiasco.

We'll see how that goes, I thought while flicking through the information on Chorwan.

Legion command knew the Sovereign Worlds were just baiting us. They didn't really care about peace, or else they would've given us the bastard as soon as he RSVPed to one of the bloodiest events in the galaxy. They wanted us out of this galaxy so they could have all the control.

Well, too fucking bad.

If they weren't going to give him to the Legion, we were just going to take him. I'd enjoy seeing what they had to say to that. Most likely they wouldn't even notice.

That was the goal.

Thankfully, my celebrity status as an invincible Rodinian gladiator was more well-known than my stealthy life as part of Legion. Chorwan wouldn't know what hit him, and this whole project could be over and I could spend the rest of my days with my beautiful mate.

Melisande.

I shivered.

A signal on my comms beeped. It was from Dorn. I quickly answered the call. It was either that or jack myself.

Focus, Ly. Mission, Ly.

"Dorn, did Cade fill you in?"

Dorn sighed. "He did. I will be arriving in the mid-afternoon."

I groaned, feeling deflated. "You'll miss the first match."

"I'll be in time for the rest," said Dorn. "This is a mission, Ly. Remember?"

I scoffed. "Yeah, yeah."

"It's not just for you to show off."

I pouted. "But I like showing off. Besides, I'm good at it."

"Ly."

"Yes, I know. Trust me, I know. This mission is important to me. It's why I told Cade in the first place."

"Once I'm there I'll get intel on Chorwan.

Don't worry too much. Just focus on finding your mate."

I smiled. I really did have the best crew. "Thanks, Dorn."

"Do you think she'll be there?"

I sighed, turning my gaze back to the city. The sun was now up and several screens blasting the tournament passed by my window. "Where?"

I heard Dorn's exasperated sigh. "At the tournament. Do you think she'll be there?"

Would she be watching the tournament? I flexed my muscles. "I don't know," I smiled, imagining locking eyes with her in the crowd, imagining her watching me in all my glory. "I guess we'll see. I should probably get my training in before my match."

Dorn scoffed. "You? Train?"

Before he cut off comms, I said, "Before I forget, thanks. For backing me up."

"You're my crew. Anytime."

The comms ended and I strode into the mini-gym of my quarters. I flicked on the virtual trainer, who started to put me through my paces. I jumped up and grabbed the bar before doing several pull-ups. I wanted to make a good impression.

If she was in the crowd I needed to win.

I STOOD ON MY TIP-TOES, PEEKING OVER THE shoulders of the tall Varons surrounding me, trying to get a good glimpse at the competitors and fans arriving for the tournament. I pitched forward, accidentally stumbling into female dressed in golden silk in front of me.

The female turned around, scowling down at me.

"Sorry," I said. All of them were so stupidly tall, I could barely see anything when they were all around me.

"What are you doing?" Isaul asked, standing on my right and eyeing me like I was an errant child.

Heat crept up my cheeks and I flattened my

feet, fiddling with a lock of hair at my cheek. I lowered my gaze. I should have realized I was annoying Isaul, but I couldn't hold back my excitement.

I attended all kinds of functions, but ones that required me to dress up during the day around respectable folk was a rare treat. Usually it was go to this club, go to that room, go to transport, wait here.

I just couldn't believe I was actually going to the Pax Tournament. It had been the talk among all the upper crust of the Sovereign Worlds. There were hovering screens all over the city advertising the magnitude of this event. Everywhere around me were towers filled with lights. Aircraft after aircraft zipped around us. The city was alight in neon with advertisements and music blaring in the background.

I had grown so used to the deafening silence of the facility. Or the classical music of the wealthy. I never got to see so much neon and fanfare.

It was amazing.

The fact that the tournament was taking place in between the two worlds of the city planet was incredible. It was available for all, poor and wealthy, to celebrate the Concord that stopped the wars between the Sovereign Worlds, and perhaps invite another collective called the Legion into their fold. This Pax was supposed to be the start of peace talks or something. At least that's what I understood from the gossip.

I watched the Rodinians leaving their aircrafts, towering over the Varons, who were already tall enough at an average of six feet. They were absolutely majestic looking with their feline grace and their exotic looks. I had never seen their kind before, but, heard enough about them from vid comms that Isaul had approved for me to watch.

He wanted me to know enough to be interesting to my clients, but not enough to actually be able to help myself.

A black light-wing landed, and I watched as Chorwan Vortu stepped off his aircraft and onto the helipad.

My heart plummet straight through my stomach.

His picture made him look like a saint.

Chorwan scanned the area with a scowl. More scars went down the length of his bulging, veiny neck. His orange hair was left as a stripe on his head, and he wore an unusually tight black shirt, showcasing more scars around his arms, with golden silk pants and large black boots.

Isaul nudge me forward, guiding me along with a hand on my hip. I pushed through the crowd, keeping my head high as if I truly was mated to Isaul.

I wore a simple white dress that was elegantly cut to accentuate my body in all the right places. It billowed around me, creating a pretty frame around me. As if he sensed me, Chorwan turned, his yellow gaze falling on me. A mix of lust and unabashed hunger flickered over his face.

I fixed a polite smile on my face, and bowed my head to him, the picture of grace and elegance that I knew Isaul preferred. "Master Chorwan Vortu," I said, my smile growing as I stared up at him. *You probably have a very small penis,* I thought, my gaze turning to his giant arms barely kept at his sides. "It is a pleasure to finally meet you."

"Ah, Chorwan," Isaul called from behind me, opening his arms wide as if to hug his client.

Chorwan scowled down at Isaul, not bothering to step forward.

Isaul's arms awkwardly lowered. He turned to

me, speaking to me with wide, angry eyes as if to say I was too far away from Chorwan.

And so, it begins. I pasted on the brightest smile I could muster and walked the final few steps to Chorwan, wrapping my arms around his.

"She is absolutely remarkable, Isaul," said Chorwan, openly leering at me. At least he didn't drool. "Better than the picture."

"I could say the same about you," I said, fluttering my lashes. I nuzzled my head against his arm, inhaling deeply. His scent reminded me of fish rotting under the sun during a hot summer's day. It made it harder to pretend he turned me on. "Your scent is exquisite," I whispered into his ear. "I could have you buried in me all day long."

Chorwan growled low in his throat and pulled me closer against him.

Isaul clapped his hands. "If she is acceptable to you, then, we have an arrangement." He glanced at me briefly, before nodding to Chorwan and disappearing back into the crowds.

I knew what that look meant. Make the client comfortable, make him feel understood him, ask him about himself, get information out of him.

The more dirt I could get on Chorwan, the

more money I made. Though, I couldn't imagine what this brute would know that would interest Isaul. Unfortunately, that wasn't my place to know.

I stroked Chorwan's arm, pressing my breasts against his exposed skin. I heard him hiss and I pointedly ignored the effect that I had on him. "What would you like, Chorwan? I can make any desire come true."

He narrowed his eyes. "Any?"

I tilted my head to the side, craning my neck. Males here seemed to really like a sexy neck tease. Some even got off on just sucking my throat. "Any."

Chorwan smiled, baring broken teeth as he cupped a callous hand around the nape of my neck and squeezed. "I might take you up on that offer. But later." He led me forward, off the helipad and onto the long, narrow bridge leading into the grand arena. "The tournament should be starting soon. I don't want to miss the opening ceremonies."

"Of course, Master."

We entered the arena, crowded with citizens that hailed throughout the Sovereign Worlds. Several returning gladiators conducted interviews and took pictures with fans. I didn't really under-stand the whole joy of watching men and women destroying each other, but I guess it was no different from any other sport.

Chorwan pulled me toward one opponent, a Varon with yellow skin and black hair. He was shorter than Chorwan, but he was still built like a beast. He wore no shirt and was currently showing off his rock-hard abs to some squealing fan girls. His green gaze caught sight of us standing there, and he smiled menacingly.

"Chorwan," the gladiator called, smiling for a picture, before stalking toward my client. "Who is this rare bird beside you?"

"This is Melisande, my khosa for the tournament." Then Chorwan addressed me. "This is Anzel Vox, a champion gladiator."

Anzel took my hand and kissed it. "What an absolute pleasure," he muttered against my flesh. "I have never seen a creature so beautiful."

I smiled prettily for the gross giant. Gotta look friendly. "It's nice to meet you, Sir Anzel. You're a returning gladiator?"

Anzel flexed his muscles. "Don't I look it?"

Gross. "Absolutely. You are quite exquisite."

Anzel waggled his eyebrows. "I could say the same about you."

Chorwan chuckled. "Anzel is quite the fighter. He'll be in the second match."

"I'll put on quite the show for you," Anzel whispered in my ear.

I stroked Chorwan's arm, hoping it would make him see how closely this Anzel stood by me. Most of the time, clients wanted to keep a khosa to themselves. Unfortunately for me, he was not getting the hint.

"Anzel believes he will be able to defeat the great Lyova Artox."

My heart stopped.

"What?" I whispered.

Lyova?

Lyova was here?

I scanned the area, looking for him in the crowds. Maybe he was having an interview or taking pictures with the fans. Did he see me? Did he know I was here?

Chorwan raised an eyebrow. "You know of Lyova Artox?"

I coughed to clear my throat. "Just heard of him. I don't actually know him."

Anzel rolled his eyes. "He is the great unde-feated Rodinian gladiator. For now. I mean, how can they be so great when the Rodinians have only competed amongst themselves?" He winked at me, his hand grazing my cheek lightly. "I'll win the battle for you, beautiful."

I stepped away from his touch but paused when I noticed Chorwan's scowl.

He was unhappy.

Unhappy clients caused problems for Isaul, and therefore, for me.

"That would be wonderful," I said, composing myself once more.

"How long are you here, you pretty thing?" Anzel asked, a finger stroking the side of my cheek.

This time I allowed it. I didn't step back. Even though he wasn't my client and it made me feel gross inside, I held my ground. After all, it was my job—my life—to keep the client happy. Touching me made him happy, so I tilted my head to the side, hoping he liked what he saw.

Was I supposed to be entertaining both of these men? Isaul would have mentioned something like that to me, as it would be part of the terms of the contract. He accounted for every little thing, not just from his harem, but from his clients.

"I am here for the tournament, so a few days," I

answered, watching as a glorious male with tawny skin and a long mane passed along my periphery.

I knew in my gut who it was.

Lyova.

I wanted to run to him, throw my arms around him, run my hands through his mane. He looked so beautiful, smiling and waving to the fans as he walked to the pits below.

His voice carried, and I heard him as clearly as if I stood next to him. It should have been impossible, given the distance. But it was almost like he spoke from inside of me.

"Thank you," Lyova said, laughing with a casual smile on his face. He seemed to glow like a Greek god walking into battle. "I hope you enjoy the tournament." He winked to his fans and walked away.

I wanted to call out to him, scream his name, but I swallowed it down.

Isaul was watching. He was always watching. And, I didn't want to think what he would do if he knew I favored such a male.

Chorwan had been speaking to me and was obviously waiting for a response. I looked at him blankly, furiously trying to recall any of the words he had said. "I'm sorry, the crowd was so loud, what did you say?"

Chorwan raised an eyebrow. "Shall we take our seats?"

Of course, the one thing I'd wanted since we had arrived, and I missed him asking me. "Yes, Master," I said, and laid my hand on his proffered arm.

I felt him shiver under my touch. "I believe you will definitely please me," said Chorwan, stroking my neck.

I nodded and let him lead me through the grand halls and toward the VIP area. We walked out into the open air of the mezzanine, the cheering crowds surrounding us as we took our seat. We had the best seat in the entire arena. The view was outstanding. It was as if we were in the gladiatorial floor itself.

I would have enjoyed the grandeur more if I didn't know that it was all coming out of my pay. That every moment of *fun* I had with my client was a moment longer I spent as an indentured servant.

I took a proffered wine glass and swallowed down in one sip. If I had to pay for it all anyway, I might as well taste what I purchased.

The spectacle of the opening ceremonies passed in a blur. I was happy that Chorwan lived up to this expectation at least. I watched the arena waiting for the whole thing to begin and that's when I saw him.

My dream champion.

Lyova.

Just thinking his name made my heart race.

The announcer's voice boomed through the speakers overhead. "Presenting, Lyova Artox!"

I watched Lyova run out from the pit. He pounced high into the sky, landing swiftly on his feet. The crowd around me cheered as he slowly rose. He unsheathed the swords at his sides, twirling them around before throwing them up into the air, emitting an incredible roar as he caught them.

My chest tightened to the point of pain watching him out there. The crowd chanted his name, and my soul echoed it inside of me. Memories of half-forgotten dreams surged to the forefront, as his name ripped from my lips at the heights of unceasing pleasure.

Chorwan chuckled at my side, breaking the spell as he pat my hand that had gripped my armrest. "He's incredible, isn't he?"

I fumbled for my drink, draining the glass once more and nodding for a refill. I watched Lyova raise his hands to the crowds, remembering how he thrust into me, how he whispered my name against my neck.

"He is extraordinary," I said, before taking another long sip of my wine.

Ah, the arena.

It was so good to be back, almost like visiting an old friend.

I twirled my sword, tossing back my mane as I raised one hand to the crowds. They still chanted my name. That was the trick. It didn't matter who you faced in the arena; it was the crowd you had to win over.

My opponent groaned behind me. I could've ended it as soon as he entered the ring. But where was the fun in that? No one liked to watch a quick match. And the people came here for a show.

And I would definitely give them a show.

My opponent roared at me from behind.

"Oh, so you're finally up," I called, turning around and watching him run at me. He swung his sword around aimlessly.

Coward. Who attacked from the behind anymore?

He swiped and I dodged.

"And The Destroyer misses," called the robot hovering above us, videoing the match in a holograph several feet in the air for those in the nosebleeds to see.

The Destroyer swung his sword again. I blocked it with my sword, the sound ringing through the arena, vibrating against me. I kicked him, pushing him back into the middle. I watched him stumble, landing pathetically on his back.

I shrugged and looked at the time.

I could wait.

I had time.

The crowd laughed, pointing as The Destroyer struggled to stand in his armor.

It would be laughable if it weren't so pathetic. I bit back laughter as I watched him roll to standing. He roared and ran at me again, swiping at me. Again.

Really, this was supposed to be returning

champions. Even if I weren't on another mission, there really should have been better competitors.

I dodged his sword easily. And who called themselves *The Destroyer* anyway? It just seemed like he was setting himself up for failure.

Maybe I should figure out a show name for myself. Maybe, Lyova the Amazing.

I dodged another swing.

No, maybe Lyova the Sex God of the Galaxies.

That was too long.

I dodged another attack, sighing and sheathing my sword. The Destroyer roared, running at me before jumping into the air. I dodged his attack and swiped my sword, gashing through his armor and into his leg.

He screamed, gripping the wound, before I kicked him, straddling him. I ripped off his helmet, tossing it in the distance before punching him in his face. He sputtered blood, his legs straining behind me, trying to kick me off him.

I gripped his neck and rested my knee against his chest, keeping him still. "Hey, now. Hold. I really need to ask you a question. It's really important, and if I don't know it will be really distracting the rest of the day." He blinked up at me as I leaned into his mottled face. The robot whirred closer, trying to capture our conversation. "So, what exactly do you destroy? I mean, really, you are terrible. The worst you could possibly destroy is carpet. Maybe."

The Destroyer roared again, but before he could do anything, I punched him in the face. Again.

"It seems like they should call you The Loud Idiot, rather than The Destroyer," I shoved a finger into my ear, mocking his roaring and growling.

The crowd loved it, their laughter echoing around me.

The Destroyer groaned under me, blood covering his face. His nose was smashed, his teeth broken. Poor guy never stood a chance. If he had known what it would be like to fight against a Rodinian, he never would have stepped up.

Traditional gladiator matches were to the death.

Here, they had an out. Three taps on the ground. He should have taken the out a long time ago.

At least I went easy on him. I needed to win to be invited to the VIP box and find my quarry. But I didn't need to break all my opponents. They weren't my enemies.

The Destroyer tapped the ground lamely three times.

"Lyova Artox wins!"

The crowd erupted in cheers, stomping their feet. The video replayed a montage of the fight as the crowd cheered for me.

"Lyova! Lyova! Lyova!"

I threw down my sword, raising my hands and running throughout the arena. Holographic flowers fell at my feet as I ran around the ring.

As I approached the VIP box, I smiled to myself. I ran faster, and launched myself into a high pounce, flipping in the air, before landing swiftly into a kneel atop the mezzanine.

I rose slowly, smirking as my name grew in volume throughout the arena. I waved to them all as if this was something I did regularly. Then, I felt a presence. It was an awareness that I was desperate to acknowledge.

I turned to find familiar green eyes staring back at me. I would know them anywhere. They were the eyes of my fate-mate. The one I'd shared unity with so strongly for three glorious nights.

I took in the female's heart-shaped face and blood-red hair. Her porcelain skin was smooth, and

I knew how soft it would be when she yielded to my touch.

My mate. *Melisande.* Just thinking her name made me hard.

There she stood, clapping mechanically even as recognition dawned on her face as well. She recognized me. A feeling of longing and desire filled me up, and I recognized it as coming from her. From our unity bond.

It was weak now and would grow in intensity when we bonded together.

And we would bond together. I would raze planets to make that happen. The fact that she already wanted to be with me as well made me want to claim her right here and now.

Finally, I realized what was wrong. She wasn't just a random spectator in the crowd. She was here with someone. Belatedly, I was conscious of the fact that there was a male that was standing way too close to her.

A savage brute of a male.

That evil bastard I was supposed to bring in.

Chorwan Vortu.

That disgusting thing leaned down to whisper something in my mate's perfect ear. She didn't respond to whatever he said to her, instead she sat stiffly at his side, folding her hands in her lap.

That was when I saw them. Ornately decorated silver cuffs wrapped around her small wrists. They were mating cuffs.

My gaze widened on those metal cuffs as realization dawned on me.

She was mated. To someone who wasn't me. I fisted my hands, rage burning within me.

What was she doing wearing mating cuffs sitting next to that murderous bastard?

I ran back into the pit where the other competitors were preparing for their next fight. I inhaled deeply, closing my eyes, trying to calm myself. She was mated. How was that possible? The universe wouldn't show me my mate, my soul, only to have her be mated to another.

I punched the wall.

They were announcing the next match. I needed to get a handle on myself, but the beast inside of me raged to be let loose. To go to that VIP box and shred Chorwan, mission be damned.

And then I would take Melisande and tell her that she belonged to me. She knew it as well as I did. She wanted to be with me.

An epiphany cleared my head. Maybe that was

what fate was trying to tell me? Maybe Melisande was trapped and needed me to kill her bond-mate? If it was Chorwan, then it would make sense. I would be fulfilling my mission for Legion command while also freeing my mate from her shackles.

The more I thought on it, the more I embraced the rising rage of my beast.

"Announcing Anzel Vox."

Someone smacked my shoulder. I whirled around and growled, seeing a yellow Varon staring up at me. "Get ready to lose, Lyova," he sneered before running out into the ring.

I scowled, my vision narrowing to pinpoints of fury. Like I'd lose to the likes of him.

"Announcing Lyova Artox."

I roared, barely containing the feral shift that threatened to take over me. It was one thing to shift into battle mode while in the field. Quite another to do so in front of the Sovereign Worlds who were more likely to be potential enemies than allies.

I exploded out of the pit, ignoring the cheers from fans. Melisande still sat in the box, watching me with those beautiful eyes. I felt that tug yet again. The one that practically begged me to save her, even though her face beheld a gentle serenity.

Fate-mates shared a deep bond. I would know if she were in danger. And though she looked healthy and happy, my heart—no, my *soul*—somehow knew that she was in trouble. I needed to save her.

First, I needed this fight to end. As in right the fuck now.

Anzel raised his weapon, but he never had a chance. I pounced, dodging his spear, grabbing it and breaking it into two pieces, throwing it to the side. Anzel stared at the broken spear in shock, glancing back and forth between me and the spear before bolting back to the pit.

The crowd laughed as I chased after him.

"No!" He shrieked, as I caught him and threw him down onto the ground. Anzel whimpered, shielding his face with one arm as he pounded the ground repeatedly with his free hand. "Stop! I give up! I give up!"

The announcer's voice boomed through the hovering robot drones. "Anzel Vox is down!"

The crowd cheered as I stood, watching as the guards helped him limp away. I didn't hear the robot announce the next opponent. I just attacked. All I could do was attack. One after another until I was panting and the ring was filled with exhausted, unmoving bodies.

"Lyova! Lyova! Lyova!"

I stalked toward the pit, ignoring the broken and beaten competitors scrambling to get out of my way.

A familiar voice cut through my rage-filled haze. "Lyova, what's the matter? This isn't you." Dorn pulled me by the arm and led me away from the others. "What the hell was that?"

I growled low, ripping my arm from his hold.

He grabbed my shoulders and shook me. "Control yourself, Reaper, or I will do it for you." Dorn's voice was low, pitched just for me, but it settled my beast. "Use your words and speak. Demolishing your opponents isn't you. You're better than that. You give the crowd what it wants. Something happened."

I both hated and loved that Dorn could be so direct. Saved time, but I also didn't want to admit that I fucked up. "My mate," I growled. I could barely speak, my beast's anger clawing up through me. I needed to move. Wanted to roar.

Dorn placed a hand on my shoulder and stared me down, and damn if that didn't work to keep the beast contained. I forget how strong Dorn could be.

There was a reason he was Reaper Two, and his quiet demeanor lulled you into forgetting that reason.

"She's mated," I spat. "And I think she's in trouble. No, I *know* she's in trouble."

Dorn shook his head. "It's impossible. She can't be mated."

I clawed at my mane, biting back the urge to tear into him. It was overwhelming. "I saw her," I growled through clenched teeth. "I saw damned mating cuffs on her."

Dorn merely shrugged. "And? Mating cuffs mean nothing when it comes to fate-mates. Just pretty jewelry, that's all. Now, I do agree on the trouble part."

I paused in my pacing. "Go on."

"It goes hand in hand with those mating cuffs. It could all be a ruse in order to move around a slave without question."

"A ruse?" Instead of relief, the red tide of anger rose once more. "You are saying that my mate could be a slave?"

Slavery was abhorrent to Rodinians. We valued freedom and autonomy. The spirit to roam and wander was ingrained in us. "This does not make me feel better, Dorn."

"Making you feel better wasn't my intent. Focusing your misplaced anger was." Dorn's piercing gaze made the hackles in my neck rise. He was challenging me, and I deserved to be put in my place. "She doesn't belong to anyone else but you. But right now, she is a captive. Instead of being angry that she might have been claimed by another, or even that she is in the company of a war criminal, be angry that some fucker enslaved her in the first place."

"Of course. You're right. I was being stupid." I felt myself shift again, the beast returning to its slumber within me. My heart was steady, beating normally as I gazed back at Dorn, who slowly released my neck. "It was a surprise. Of course, she is my priority. Her wellbeing and safety are the most important."

"Your mate comes first. Always."

I chuckled. "Well, ladies first, that's a given," I said.

"I see you're back to normal," he said.

"Oh please, as if you didn't dangle that line for me to pick up." I started pacing again. "They're getting smarter, aren't they? The Kridrins. We'd suspected they found other means to get what they need. Just couldn't figure out how."

It was Dorn's turn to look defeated. He'd been working double time trying to coordinate with Legion command and his network of double agents to find out if the Kridrin were still abducting females for their experiments. Legion command sent a protective detail near Terra Prime—Earth— since they seemed to like human females the best, but there was nothing.

All the Reapers were out there collecting anything useful they could find, and the trail went cold almost overnight.

"Now we can surmise that some of their movements have been through legitimate channels. And it's looking like the Sovereign Worlds may have a part to play in all this."

If that were true, we needed to get that damned Chorwan more than ever. He had been picked up as a known war criminal but also as a smuggler. He had somehow escaped from a Legion holding cell in Legion-controlled space. The tech that would have been required to get him out was beyond anything the Sovereign Worlds would have in their arsenal. Suspiciously so.

And yet, here we were, playing at peace at a Pax Tournament. Rodinians knew how to walk in the shadows and still catch their prey.

My name boomed throughout the speakers. "Lyova Artox!"

Dorn leaned against the wall behind him, nodding at the arena with a soft smile. "They just announced the winners. You should get back out there, Mr. Undefeated Champion."

I almost forgot about my cover. It seemed almost petty compared to what needed to be done. A means to the end, I told myself. This was all a means to an end.

And the end I wanted was attached to Melisande.

I raised my hands, walking toward the roar of the crowd and the blood-stained arena. As I took my bows, I looked toward the VIP box. Melisande was no longer there.

I hated the feeling that came over me, but Dorn's words came back to mind. My anger needed to be focused on finding the one who enslaved my mate in the first place.

The robot congratulated all the winners and handed each of us a chip.

It was an invitation.

"We hope to see you at the wonderful winner's circle tonight."

I stared down at the chip, raising my hand to

the cheering crowds. This was why I was here. Chorwan would be on the list for the winner's circle. And with him, Melisande.

If she was there, I could get her out, and she could be free.

Lyova was amazing.

Breathtaking. Everything about him captivated me. The way he moved. The way he fought. The way he stalked each opponent.

God, I almost wanted him to come at me like that.

I glanced over at Chorwan, scowling after he lost his bet. I didn't understand why he bet against Lyova. The odds were enormous. Now, he was sulking.

A sulking client did not pay well. Especially not a sulking client who had just lost a big bet.

I stroked Chorwan's arm. "This tournament is so exciting, I'm glad you invited me along," I whispered into his ear. "It's my first time seeing gladiators." He turned toward me, his yellow eyes lingering on my lips. That was a good sign. At least he was acknowledging my existence again.

His thumb stroked my lower lip.

I quickly turned away. I didn't need him to be that happy. Just enough for him to stop sulking.

"Shall we go, my dear?" Chorwan tugged on my arm.

I fought back a sigh. My attention worked too well. I knew I needed to entertain him, but my gaze lingered on Lyova. The arena was abuzz with his name, and the thought of leaving him twisted my gut.

"Are you sure?" I asked, hesitating as Chorwan tugged my arm once more. "Weren't you just telling me how much you enjoyed these fights?" If Lyova won enough of his matches, he would be invited to the winner's circle. I would be able to see him. Chorwan and I were on the guest list.

Just being able to say hello to him would be enough.

"I already know how the fight will end," Chorwan shrugged. "It's not enjoyable watching opponents so outmatched." A coy smirk split his face and I shuddered at what he could possibly be thinking. "I would like to spend some more time with you." He pulled me close to his body, his rotten breath suffocating me. "Alone."

I stopped myself from gagging.

Yep, it was definitely time to go to work.

I fixed my practiced smile on my face and stood. Another cheer erupted from the crowd and I quickly glanced back, watching as Lyova dodged another attack, pouncing high into the sky before tackling his opponent to the ground.

"Why don't we just finish this match?"

Chorwan scowled. "I didn't think Isaul employed such rude escorts."

At the use of Isaul's name, I immediately turned and straightened my posture. Once again, I nearly forgot I was being watched on surveillance. And I didn't need this jerk complaining to Isaul about my inability to keep him happy.

"Excuse me," I said, wrapping my arms around his while my other hand played with his shirt buttons. "I thought you would enjoy a female who understood the love of a good battle." I lowered my eyes, puckering my lips, something I practiced in the mirror in order to appear sultry. "I meant no offense."

Chorwan chuckled patting my hand as he led us out of the arena and through the neon tunnels.

"You can make it up to me. You said I could have anything I desire, right?"

"Of course."

I followed him through the alleys of the arena. There were several other escorts sitting on black sofas, whispering into their clients' ears, stroking their legs and arms. One winked at me as she led her client into a room. A couple kissed in the shadows, the male hiking up her skirt.

Only months of practice allowed me to keep my disgust from showing on my face. I knew what would be coming soon. Sure, this happened to me all the time, but that didn't make it better.

Chorwan nuzzled my neck. "Should we be like them," he whispered in my ear, nodding to the couple going at it. His hand touched my ass, grabbing it lightly before his teeth were at my neck. I gasped. Not from pleasure, but because I knew it was what he wanted. His hand cupped my sex and he whirled me around, locking his lips with mine. "I want you."

"You can have me," I whispered, slowly pushing him away. "But would you want me on display, or private, just for you?" I quickly added.

Chorwan pulled away frowning, but despite

his annoyance he nodded and led me to his quarters deep within the arena.

The room was large and dark just like the rest of this place with a massive bed and a table at the center with a vase of flowers. There were tall flowers decorating the corners, and a nice hovering chandelier above the bed.

I looked around awkwardly, holding my hands in front of me "How does one afford such an extravagant place?" I asked, hoping he would at least spill some information Isaul could use.

"I'm not in the mood to talk," said Chorwan, spinning me around. His lips were on mine, his tongue forcing its way into my mouth. His hands cupped my breasts, but all I could think of was how I wished he was another.

Lyova.

I moaned. Thinking of him touching me, thrusting into me.

God, I wished he were here.

Chorwan took my goblet and kissed my neck lightly. "Why don't you go freshen up while I pour you another glass?"

I wiped my mouth and went into the bathroom, locking the door behind me. My lipstick was smeared. I took some paper to tidy up the edges.

No matter what I did, my skin was still pink from where the lipstick stained it.

I splashed water on my face, trying to calm the heat racing up my neck.

You can do this, I told myself, staring into my tired green eyes. It's just like all the other times before.

Except, Lyova was real. He wasn't just my dream champion.

He was a real champion. And the thought of being with anyone else other than him made me sick.

He recognized me. I knew he did. It wasn't just some silly dream I made up to give me hope during these dark times.

Tears spilled down my cheeks. I bit back a sob.

"Melisande?"

I cleared my throat and wiped my eyes. Regardless of what I felt, this was my reality. I needed to power through this moment. Just this once, and then I would be able to be with Lyova again in the evening. Somehow, I would meet him alone and tell him how I felt about him.

Maybe there was a chance that he wouldn't think I was batshit crazy.

But first: survive.

"Coming," I called.

I ran my hands through my hair and practiced my best adoring smile. My eyes were still bloodshot from crying, but at least my skin wasn't splotchy any longer. Besides, clients usually focused on one thing and one thing only.

He wouldn't notice if I was smiling.

When I returned, Chorwan handed me another glass of sparkly liquid, and I chugged the contents.

He chuckled, setting the glass back onto the table. "I guess you were thirsty."

"Very," I nodded, dabbing at my mouth.

I sat on the bed, looking around at the beautiful golden lights, illuminating the room. If it wasn't for my circumstances, this would be quite romantic.

The room began to blur around me.

I blinked several times, wondering if it was just the lighting.

The world around me tilted.

"Are you all right, my dear?" Chorwan asked, as he pushed my hair back, kissing my shoulder. His voice sounded so far away.

I leaned into his touch, moaning and closing my eyes.

I was so exhausted.

My eyes shot open and I tried to stand. Something was wrong. I moved toward the door, but my legs weren't working properly. I stumbled into the table, the vase of flowers spilling and shattering on the floor.

What was happening?

I slipped from the table to the floor, feeling my vision waver. I crawled toward the door, the broken shards from the vase dug into my skin, scratching and drawing blood.

I heard footsteps. I looked up and saw Chorwan towering above me. He chuckled, kneeling down, and swooping me into his arms. "Where do you think you're going, pretty bird?"

The door opened and Anzel appeared. There were two of him, flickering in and out from each other His face was a mess of scratches. His nose was bandaged and there were bandages around his neck.

"Did anyone see you?" Chorwan asked.

Anzel shook his head, his gaze turning to mine before a terrible smile broke over his face. "I see you had no trouble?"

Chorwan chuckled. "None whatsoever."

"No," I muttered, trying to push away from Chorwan's hold.

I was being deposited on the bed. Anzel hovered over my body, his fingers pulling at my dress.

"No," I struggled against him, tears spilling down. I tried to hit him, but my arms weren't listening to me.

"Ssshhh," Anzel hushed, grabbing my hands with his and holding me tight against him. He turned to Chorwan. "She doesn't want it, Chorwan."

Chorwan chuckled. "She will."

Anzel kissed my neck and I whimpered, trying to push him away. He sighed. "I can't fuck her if she isn't into it."

Chorwan sighed and grabbed something from his desk drawer. It was a small vial filled with blue liquid. "Feed her this," he said, handing the vial to Anzel. "She'll be begging for you once it hits her bloodstream."

These motherfuckers. I struggled against him, but Anzel shoved the vial in my mouth, making me down the contents. "It's okay, beautiful."

I gagged. A strange feeling came over me. Everything around me felt hot. I leaned against Anzel. I had no control over my body. I held onto him as the whole world seemed to blur and morph around me; as if the world around me was tilting and flying away. I touched my mouth to see if it was still there, the feeling making me giggle.

I lifted my gaze to Anzel. His blue eyes shifted to gold. His hair grew into a beautiful long mane.

"Lyova," I whispered, taking his face into my hands.

"What the fuck?" He shouted. "I'm not Lyova."

I didn't care. I pressed my lips against his, my tongue running along the seam of his mouth, seeking entrance. He moaned when I captured his tongue, and sucked it inside of me.

He pulled away from me, smirking as I pulled at his shirt. His golden eyes shifted back to blue and Anzel's face appeared once again.

"No," I moaned, falling back and hitting the floor. I groaned, not able to move anymore, giving up. "I can't do this anymore," I whimpered, nuzzling into the floor and closing my eyes.

THE DOORS TO THE GRAND HALL OPENED AND an array of twinkling holographic stars and cande-labras shaped like planets hovered above the crowd. The citizens of the Sovereign Worlds dressed in sparkling dark garments, all the better to display their own bright coloring. The Rodinian delegates easily stood out among the crowd as they mingled with dignified elegance.

They were the perfect ambassadors for the Legion. Beautiful, noble, and ridiculously wealthy, they were everything that the Sovereign Worlds valued and envied, especially the peoples of Varonis Prime.

It was why I had been chosen as the perfect Reaper for this assignment, and yet all I could think about was Melisande. Where in star's blazes was she?

Cade and Talus were always going on about their mating bonds, and how they were able to feel their respective fate-mates through it. Yet, the only thing I felt was the worry twisting in my gut.

Dorn stood by me, playing at being the delighted guest as he listened to some Varon senator ramble on about the architecture of the building. Though Reaper Two liked knowing random trivia, even he needed to pluck a nearby goblet from a passing servant's tray. Dorn knew his role, though, and continued to deflect any distractions so I could stay on mission.

The servant offered me a drink, but I declined. I needed to be at my most witty and charming for Melisande. Scanning the room for my mate's fiery red hair, I waved at a few familiar faces from the VIP box. A few smiled and waved in my direction before returning to their conversation.

Melisande was not here.

I whispered into my comms so Dorn could hear me though he was barely six feet from me. "I don't see Chorwan Vortu." His ugly face would have stood out in all this beauty. Strange since all VIP members were invited to this gig. It was an honor that no one would want to miss.

Beside the exclusive invite, Chorwan was a known fan of the tournaments and the competitors. Rubbing shoulders with the elite and powerful was right in his wheelhouse.

A terrible feeling settled over me, like cold fingers walking down my spine. I ignored it, though. There were a multitude of reasons why both Melisande and Chorwan could be delayed.

Traffic.

Bathroom emergency.

Wardrobe malfunction.

Chorwan tripped and fell crotch first into a pit of spikes.

I smiled at that image.

Dorn thrust a glass of a sparkling drink into my face. "Whatever you're thinking about, stop. You'll creep out the guests."

I growled at him. "If they're all right seeing you, then they have nothing to fear from me." Still, I snatched the proffered glass and downed it in one swallow.

The liquid burned going down my throat and left a vile taste in my mouth. "What the hell, this is awful," I winced.

Dorn raised a brow. "You just raved about this damned vintage not ten minutes ago, which by the way, was brought here by some people you know."

I followed his gaze to a Rodinian couple walking toward us. They were dressed in the black and gold robes of House Trivani from Rodinia Prime. "The Ambassador herself is here?" She was a regal lady with braids taming her flowing mane that rippled down her back. The male beside her was her heart-mate and as feral a warrior as I'd ever had the pleasure to battle alongside.

I couldn't help but tug on my suit just a bit in the face of her stoic bearing.

Dorn slapped a hand on my shoulder. "I'll do a lap while you do your thing. Comms on." With that, Reaper Two slipped into the shadows.

The noble lady dipped into a quick curtsy while the male at her side bowed.

I returned their greeting, carefully averting my gaze so my attention landed on the male rather than his mate. "Lord and Lady Trivani. How are you enjoying the tournament?"

"We are enjoying it indeed! You bring great honor to your noble house, Lyova, especially during these unusual times."

I received Lord Trivani's praise with a nod. To

anyone listening, it would seem that he was praising my undefeated streak, but I knew better. He had served as a Legion Reaper, as was required by all able-bodied Rodinian males. It was a point of pride that we never speak of our service among outsiders.

Our value to the Legion collective was in reconnaissance and apprehension. Hiding in plain sight was one of our favorite games.

"We are placing our bets on you," Lady Trivani said. "We shall be staying with the rest of the delegation until the closing ceremonies. If you need anything, don't hesitate to call."

Her mate handed me a comm chip. "That is very generous of you, Lady. I will make note of it. Though, I would be tempted to call in this favor in order to see *you* fight in the arena."

Lady Trivani had once been a terrifying fighter in her heyday as a beloved bellatrix. She flashed a knowing smile toward her mate who chuckled even as he laid a sweet kiss on her cheek. "Those days are far behind me, Lyova, but I do delight in your charm. To Lyova Artox." The Trivanis raised their glasses to me, and I followed suit, raising mine.

I took the smallest sip from it I could muster. Dorn was right, this was one of my favorite wines, and yet something about it was off. Or, perhaps I was the one off. My stomach was tying itself into knots. I felt uneasy. Tainted. Like I was going to vomit all over this glistening, pretty floor.

A sickening feeling of dread shivered over me. These weren't my feelings. It was Melisande. It had to be.

I was feeling her through our bond. It was too new; I hadn't known what to look for. "Dorn, we need out. I think Melisande's in trouble."

"Have you seen them?"

"No, but I just realized that I'd be been feeling her through our bond after all."

Dorn muttered dark curses. "Head to the northside exit. We'll plan there." His rage helped to keep me calm. Devolving into a battle frenzy would likely be frowned upon especially among the upper crust of the Sovereign Worlds.

I needed to think. The only thing I could feel from my bond was a sharp twisting in my gut. I hoped on all the ancient gods that it wasn't a literal knife in my mate's belly I was feeling.

No, fate wouldn't be so cruel as to reveal my beautiful mate only to have her die in such a way. Alone and helpless.

Rodinians have used their bonds to communicate with their mates. The Trivanis were having an entire conversation with barely any words spoken between them, and they were heart-mates. Fate-mates would have an even deeper bond that went deeper than flesh.

I imagined her. Melisande. Her hair. Her eyes. Her voice. The way she called my name in the throes of ecstasy.

Something like mists parted in my mind, but I didn't see my mate. Instead I saw Chorwan Vortu's leering face wavering in front of me.

I saw red and moved to strike, when I felt arms brace around me and pin me against a column. "Quiet." Dorn's voice was pitched low, but it was the slice of command in it that my beast responded to.

There was a reason that he was Reaper Two in the field.

I nodded, letting him know that my beast was firmly leashed. He backed away from me and saw that he had barely needed to flex his strength. I shook my head. I might be the undefeated gladiator in the arena, but Reaper captains were on a whole different level.

Dorn put a finger to his lips and nodded toward two socialites nearing our vicinity. Two

Varon ladies holding goblets, dressed in hues of blue and gold. They were similar, appearing as twins, with cropped short hair and blue shadow all around the eyes. He had his gauntlet angled toward them, and I tapped my comms to listen in on what he was hearing.

"Did you see that lovely khosa in the VIP box today? I hadn't seen her race before."

"All the races tend to whirl in my mind, too. Look her up on your link, would you? The Sovereign Worlds expands so quickly now. It would be lovely if the Rodinian delegation defects from that awful Legion and decides to join us. Wouldn't their world be a lovely treat to visit? I hear they still have protected jungles on Rodinia Prime."

"Oh yes," said one, drinking from her goblet. "I believe the khosa is called Human, from a Terran colony, I suppose. She's clearly done well for herself. That brute of a client of hers must be paying her well. She had the most beautiful hair I've ever seen. I expected to see her here actually, to ask about her spa treatments."

"I saw her enter his chambers," the other waggled her eyebrows. "Apparently, a random gladiator entered as well. Anzel somebody. The one who lost to that delightful Lyova Artox."

"Everyone loses to Lyova Artox."

I didn't need to hear the rest. Blood boiled in my veins and I sprinted from the room.

I heard Dorn shout behind me, but I ignored him. I had no time. Who knew what was happening now?

I clamped my eyes closed, feeling through myself. Reaching for that bond, I let it lead me to Melisande.

"You sense her nearby?" Dorn said through our comms, more a statement than a question.

"Yes," I said, not bothering to look back. "She's in trouble."

I followed the perimeter of the arena toward the luxury suites on the prime side of the building. It boasted a lovely view of the glittering city above the clouds.

But the only view I cared to see was Chorwan's blood splattering the walls.

Two guards with crossed arms stood flanking a doorway. I knew it was the one I needed. I didn't think, I attacked.

I tore flesh from bone, not bothering to see where the parts lay. Dorn could finish whatever was left behind. I threw myself against the door and burst through in a rain of splintering wood.

Chorwan, that fucking bastard, sat upon a chair gripping his cock as he watched Anzel climb atop my mate.

Anzel turned toward us with wide eyes, his ass cheeks bare with his pants around his knees. He hovered above Melisande, who rested on the bed with eyes closed, arms splayed as if she had fallen. Her dress was torn down the middle, exposing everything to his unworthy gaze.

I would pluck out his eyes and present them to my mate as a bonding gift.

In a blur of movement, I pounced on Anzel, tearing him off Melisande and throwing him into the wall. I imagined exposing his beating heart and ripping it away from the ruin of his chest, but Melisande needed me more. The bond between us called to me and wouldn't relent until I'd scooped her into my arms.

Cradling her naked body against me, I breathed in her scent. Beneath the chemical additives of artificial perfumes and other cosmetic enhancements, she was there, faint but alive. "Melisande," I murmured against her temple. "Melisande, please wake up."

"Ly, we need to go." Dorn stepped through the broken doorway a blaster trained on Chorwan, who had barely tucked himself away.

The war criminal fumbled for the blaster on his belt, finally brandishing it, trying to decide who to aim for.

If he were smart, he would aim for me.

He aimed at Dorn.

"Look, if you want the girl, take her," Chorwan said. "She's paid for."

I bared my teeth, a warning growl ripping through the air, startling Chorwan.

"Actually," Dorn said in his deadpan tone, "we're here for you."

I had the satisfying moment of seeing a whole range of expressions flickering over his face before settling on confusion. "You're what?"

"Chorwan Vortu, you are hereby detained by the Legion. We have questions."

And with that, Chorwan bellowed with rage, throwing himself onto Dorn.

Dorn used the other male's momentum to hurl him into the hallway. He landed into the wall with a sickening crunch.

Anzel moaned from the floor, slowly standing. "Chorwan?"

"He's kind of occupied for the moment," I said. I wanted to see him bleed, but Melisande's care was more important to me, and something inside of me just knew that she needed me close. Even now, it seemed like color was coming back into her cheeks. "Say, I've kind of got my hands full, so why don't you do me a favor and tell me what you drugged my mate with. I'll let you keep your arms attached to your body."

Anzel's face drained from a mottled gray to a pale white. "I had nothing to do with that. It was all Chorwan! He said it was okay! He said that Reene owed him."

"Owed him? For what?" Dorn asked.

"I don't know—" Anzel started, then was cut off when a hail of laser blasts cut through the room. One of the shots hit Anzel right in the shoulder, whirling him around.

We took cover. I tucked Melisande against my body. "Dorn?" I shouted.

"Clear. He's bolting. I'll go after him."

"I'm coming with you."

"What about your mate?"

"I'm not leaving her here. The safest place for her to be is right here in my arms."

Dorn spared me a glance before nodding.

Then he charged out of the room and I was one step behind him with Melisande cradled safely against me.

"Fuck, I really wish you would've shot him," I muttered over comms as I urged my legs to run faster. Sure, it was great he shot Anzel, hopefully some place that hurt a lot.

"We can't kill him," Dorn gasped, gaining ground on me. "Orders. Intel."

My beast roared at that. The bastard was the mastermind behind Melisande's near-rape. "Do you really think we need to gather intel on him now when he's trying to kill us?"

Dorn ran up next to me, scowling. "I am not arguing with you."

Fine. We would bring him in. Alive. Delivered to Legion command with a big, pretty bow.

And once they were done with him, I would get to skin him while he screamed.

Gunshots zipped past us, waking me from my reverie. I dodged bullet after bullet, but this hall was never ending. I needed to get her to my quarters, but they were too far away. I needed to fight if we were going to escape this in one piece.

I paused, recognizing the area from the previous day. This was where we were welcomed.

The pit was close. The pit would be a good place. There were so many lockers and shelves to hide inside. I could hide her. I turned right, running through the foyer of the arena before following the ramp down.

"Where are you going?" Shouted Dorn.

"The pit!"

"What? Why?"

"Just trust me."

I kicked open the doors, stumbling through the room. I scanned it, looking for the best spot, before resting her under several benches. "It's going to be all right," I whispered in her ear. "I'm going to get you out of this." I stroked her cheek, kissing her forehead, before covering the bench with a long tarp.

Dorn pressed his body into the shadows, holding his blaster at the ready. I waited in the shadows near the entrance. I inhaled deeply, allowing red to consume my vision, allowing my beast to take over my body.

I was going to rip this asshole into shreds.

Legion command could go fuck themselves for all I cared.

I heard Chorwan's footsteps in the distance. "Lyova!" He shouted. "Give me the girl and you can live."

I saw his shadow slowly coming down the ramp. And I waited. I pressed myself deeper into the shadows, watching as his giant body filled the entrance. He stomped into the room with untied boots, a large blaster at his side. His form reeked of strength and pride.

I crouched low in the darkness.

"We could always share her, you and I," Chorwan sneered.

"I don't share, you bastard," I growled before pouncing.

I landed on him, my legs wrapping around his face as my teeth dug into his neck. Chorwan shrieked, his hands clawing to pull me off. His legs stumbled into benches and he slammed me into the lockers, but I held on.

He was strong, but I was stronger.

I locked my arm around him, punching him in the face, and digging my nails into his eyes. He screamed, trying to grab at his face. I released him for a moment, watching him stumble before grabbing him and throwing him into the lockers.

He was going to hurt my mate.

I grabbed him by the throat and threw him

across the room. He scrambled to get out of the way, crawling toward the entrance, whimpering.

He was going to watch as someone defiled her. While she was passed out.

I picked him up by his hair. I wrapped my arms around his neck, pushing and pulling.

"Wait!" I heard Dorn shout, but I didn't care.

There was a snap and Chorwan went limp in my arms.

"Please tell me he's still alive." Dorn groaned, putting away his blaster. He strode toward Chorwan's limp body, kneeling down and pressing his fingers into his neck. He sighed, shaking his head. "He's dead, Ly."

I shrugged. "Oops."

Dorn looked heavenward, shaking his head as he took a long, deep breath. "You kill the male we're supposed to get intel on and all you can say is 'oops'? Legion command is going to be pissed."

"Legion command can die for all I care," I growled, reaching down to gently grab my mate.

It felt so good having her in my arms again. I pressed my forehead into hers, inhaling her scent, allowing it to soothe the beast away.

"We should get her back to our quarters," said Dorn. Melisande moaned, turning over in my arms.

I nodded, stroking her cheek. "Yeah."

I followed Dorn out of the pit, my eyes imprisoned by Melisande's sleeping form. I was able to get her away from the big bad war criminal, but if she was sold to the bastard, obviously she was owned by someone else.

Who had her? And what did I need to do to get her free?

I OPENED MY EYES, SEEING BRIGHT GOLDEN lights cast on a white ceiling. I knew something was off. Something terrible had happened. I grimaced, allowing the memories to return, to sink in.

I whimpered, remembering Chorwan blurring, the goblet dropping from my hands as the world tilted. I remembered Chorwan opening the door and Anzel entering the rooms, pushing me down on the bed.

They'd given me drugs.

I clamped my eyes shut. I didn't want to remember. But the dam was already open, and despite my urges, the memories returned one after another.

I remembered giggling, Anzel transforming

into Lyova and then turned back to Anzel again. I remembered the world going black, yet still I felt my skirts being pushed up. I felt his lips at my neck.

And then...

And then...

I sniffed, inhaling deeply to calm myself. I bit back a sob, biting my tongue in my attempts to keep silent. A raspy, squeaky sound escaped my lips, sounding like a pathetically wounded animal.

But I was pathetic.

Why hadn't I been more careful?

I should have expected something like this to happen. It never had before, and that I was thankful for. Still, men who bought and paid for these types of things were never to be trusted. I wondered why Chorwan didn't just ask for it in his price. I would do whatever he wanted. It's not like I hadn't done threesomes before.

I just never had it forced on me.

I always knew what I was getting into when it came to a gig.

Isaul explained to me what a client wanted. What their dreams and yearnings were. I shivered, imagining what next torture Chorwan would put me through.

I wiped the tears from my eyes. I didn't want to open them. I didn't want to see Anzel and Chorwan standing there. I didn't want to know what they would do to me next.

Now that I was taking stuck, my body didn't seem so beaten up. I opened an eye, looking at my arms and hands. I wasn't bruised. My body still felt... intact. I didn't feel violated. Maybe they didn't?

Or maybe I was in shock?

"Ly, she's awake."

Ly?

I opened my eyes, sitting up and looking around at a completely different room. It was grander than Chorwan's. The bed was enormous. I was covered in a large white blanket and completely surrounded by pillows. There was a small, quaint tea set across from me, sitting on a round table with beautiful flowers. A window to my left displayed a lovely view of the city. The sun cast golden hues against the glistening metal.

Just how long had I been knocked out?

In front of me, beyond the table, were open doors connecting to what appeared to be a living room. Someone with dark skin that was nearly purple paced back and forth. Even farther were more connecting doors to what I could only assume was another bedroom.

If these weren't Chorwan's quarters, where was I?

A part of me worried I was in Anzel's rooms.

I shivered, grabbing the blanket and holding it close to my chest.

A familiar male strode toward me through the living room, his golden eyes filled with worry. His tawny skin stretched taut over rippling muscles as his long legs crossed the distance between us. "Are you all right?"

My heart thundered within me. Lyova. He was here. He was here with me.

I wanted to call his name. I wanted to cry and wrap my arms around him.

But Isaul was watching.

Isaul was always watching.

I wiped my eyes, already feeling more tears welling and threatening to fall. "I'm fine," I sniffed. "Where am I?"

"In my quarters," he said.

"And mine," called the purple male from the living room. "I'm Dorn." He smiled and waved at me before turning his attention back to his tablet.

"How long have I been... out?"

Lyova stroked my hand with his thumb. "All night. You were drugged."

I nodded. "I remember." I stroked his mane and he pressed his face into the palm of my hand, purring lightly.

It soothed me. Everything about him made me feel calm.

"How much do you remember?" He asked, pulling himself up and sitting next to me on the bed. His hand was still in mine, the other coming around me, pulling me closer to him.

I sighed, rubbing my forehead. "Too much." I sniffed again, feeling the waterworks already brewing. God, I wished I was better than this. I didn't want him to think I was such a cry baby, but every time I thought of Anzel or Chorwan, I remembered the world tilting and being pushed down on the bed. "It'll probably haunt my dreams decades from now."

He stroked my hair. "I'm sorry I didn't come sooner."

"It's fine." Speaking was becoming difficult. I tried to work my lips to ask the question. They trembled. It was difficult to form words, but I had to know. "Did anything," I sniffed, blinking back tears, "did anything happen?"

Lyova shook his head, pulling the blanket up to my chin. "No. I came in time." He kissed my forehead.

I nodded, feeling the tears immediately leave me. I broke into a sob, covering my face with both hands as I turned away from him. I didn't want him to see. I didn't want him to know how broken I was. How pathetic I was.

Lyova pulled me into him, allowing me to bury my face into his chest as I cried. I sobbed loudly. Chorwan still lingered deep in my mind, haunting me. Even knowing he wasn't able to torture me; he and Anzel weren't able to have their way with me, just made everything terrible come crashing down on me. If Lyova hadn't come, if he hadn't saved me, I would still be in that room. They would still be tormenting me.

Isaul was watching.

Quickly, I wiped my tears and pushed Lyova away. If this continued, Isaul would know something strange was happening between me and Lyova. Well, there was something completely strange happening. Who dreamt of a beautiful, sexy man and then met him in real life? A man I felt completely and utterly tied to in no way I'd ever imagined.

It was completely weird. Maybe Isaul didn't believe in such things.

But if he did, he would find out and take me far away. Knowing Isaul, he would hide me deep in the galaxy where Lyova could never find me.

Lyova kissed my head, kissed my cheek. His purring increased and he laced his fingers with mine. His whole body warmed me, but if Isaul saw...

"Please stop," I whispered, taking my hands from him and putting distance between us. My heart cracked at the words. I didn't want to push him away. I didn't want him to leave me, but I needed to protect him.

I needed to protect us.

Emotion flickered over Lyova's face before a calm mask took over. I didn't like seeing him hurt, but it was better this way. Instead of pushing for answers, he respected my words. He pulled himself away from me, standing up to give us more distance; taking my heart with him.

"You need to be careful," I whispered, trembling. I felt so cold. Maybe it was a side effect from the drugs. I needed to be quick. There was a lag time in recording, usually while I was inactive. No reason to record when I was doing boring things.

"He can hear you. See you." I pointed to the common injection sites behind my ear, my shoulder, the bend at my elbow.

Understanding dawned in his eyes. "Bots?"

I nodded, not daring to say more. "Everywhere. Take care what you say." I needed him to believe me. Needed him to know that I wasn't rejecting him. Would never reject him.

Lyova apprised me with those golden eyes of his, and it was like he blazed a trail into my very soul. Slowly, he traced the outline of my face. "You're so beautiful," he murmured before capturing my lips in a sweet kiss.

My heart pounded in my chest, threatening to burst free. There would be no way of feigning sleep now. Somewhere in his high tower, Isaul Reene would know that I've awakened, and would be checking in on my activities.

What would he think of what Chorwan had done to me? I shuddered at the dark memories that clouded my mind. I didn't want to think on them, not while I was with Lyova.

Lyova pulled the blankets more securely around my body. "You're cold. Let's get you something hot to drink. Tea? I have darjara on the warmer? Or I could hunt down some other drink if you prefer?"

I preferred to be wrapped in his arms, but I bit my lip against speaking my mind. "Darjara is fine, thank you," I said in my perfect kosha tones.

The tea service on the table was impeccable. I'd been with enough elite clients to know how much a simple-looking spread like that was worth. The tea leaves would be perfect and crisp, I could smell how fresh it was from here.

He served me my tea, and it was the first time in my life that I remember ever being served in bed. "Thank you," I repeated. I took a tentative sip, and just as I'd expected, it was tea of the highest quality. More expensive than the finest wines.

Lyova balanced on the edge of the bed, taking care not to jostle the liquid in my hands. "This entire suite is yours." He indicated a doorway. "I took the liberty of ordering some things. The concierge assured me that whatever you need would be available for you."

I didn't know what to say. "You shouldn't have gone through the trouble. My m—" I didn't want to refer to Isaul as my mate, despite what the cuffs on my wrists symbolized. "Master Reene wouldn't want you to trouble yourself on my account."

As if he read my mind, he wrapped his fingers around my right wrist. "Is he the one who gave you these?" His tone was lighthearted, but it was as if I could feel his rage simmering just under my skin.

I nodded, and his gaze sharpened.

All of him seemed to grow larger, harder, more feral. I should have been scared, especially when claws lengthened from his fingertips even as his hands morphed. His eyes gleamed with a monstrous light, and his fangs grew longer, curling over his bottom lip. An ominous rumbling sounded in the room, and I realized it came from Lyova.

I should have been scared, but I wasn't. Instead, I fought a desperate urge to curl onto his lap and sink my fingers into his riotous mane.

From one blink to the next, the growls turned into a seductive purr. I'd heard rumors of the beasts that Rodinians carried within them, but I had no idea they would be... hot.

A light knock at the door broke the spell between us. Lyova rolled his eyes and grumbled in such a boyish way that it made me giggle. "Who's that?" I asked.

"Dorn. You could say he was my business manager. Anyway, I will have to talk to Dorn, but I promise to help you," he said, patting my hand. "To get back to your master, of course."

He winked, tucking the blankets more securely around my body, before striding into the living room, closing the door behind him.

I nestled into my nest of blankets and sighed, taking another sip of the darjara tea and looking out the window. The sun was already up, and I could pretend that I was with Lyova, and Isaul would never be able to find me while I was here.

THE DOOR CLICKED CLOSED BEHIND ME. I leaned against it, closing my eyes as I knocked my head against the wood. Her scent was faint, sweet, tantalizing even given the closed door, and already I wanted to return to her. I wanted to be at her side. I wanted to cradle her in my arms as she recovered from the treatment she'd received at Chorwan's hands.

That fucking bastard.

Snapping his neck felt good.

Real good.

I shouldn't have killed him so quickly. I should have drawn out his punishment some more for what he did to Melisande.

And Anzel. As soon as I hunted down that

worthless male, I was going to peel the flesh off his bones.

My claws dug into the door. I inhaled deeply, calming myself. I was already halfway to changing into my battle form. If I wasn't careful, I would go into a frenzy, and I didn't need to be tearing up the place when Melisande was in the next room.

I threw myself down onto the couch and watched Dorn pace back and forth as he talked with Cade on comms. He met my gaze and clicked a button on his gauntlet. I was treated to the full blast of Cade's snarls.

"How dead is he?" Cade asked in a lethal whisper.

"Dead," Dorn said. "Beyond the help of repair pods. There wouldn't have been enough of him intact to scoop into one of Legion command's scorpio chairs."

I scoffed. "Besides, they'd need a head to plug their device into, and that was one of the first things I crushed."

Cade growled between clenched teeth. "Not helpful, Lyova. This mission is fucked unless you can come up with some solutions."

I raked my hands through my mane. This would be all my fault, too. I knew my mate had been out here, knew that she would have been close given how intense our unity dreams were. I just never imagined this level of hunger. How much my body would be pushing me to be with her.

I was going to have to tear into Cade and Talus for not sharing that tidbit. Lust I could handle. This was beyond that. It was like fighting to breathe after being trapped underwater.

And I couldn't even tell her anything because she'd been shot up with surveillance bots.

Bots.

Maybe there was a way to salvage this.

"I got it!"

Dorn and Cade had been hashing things out and were suddenly silent. This was a first. I wasn't used to supplying needed intel to a mission. "Melisande said that she was bugged. Something about surveillance bots in her body courtesy of her master, Isaul Reene." It killed me to even speak his name. "Everything she does is bugged and uploaded to some facility. Now, how much do you want to bet that Reene has way more intel than even Chorwan might have had?"

Dorn snapped his fingers. "Of course! Chorwan had to have gotten here somehow. He tapped someone with connections. Networks. Someone like this Isaul Reene, who uses chattel like Melisande to be his eyes and ears on anything that has worth. Look at the tournament. Where was Melisande? In the VIP Box. Doesn't matter what Chorwan knew or talked about. She would have easily been in the presence of those who had power. Senators. Law makers. Ambassadors. Even our own delegates could have been bugged."

"They're too smart to say anything of value," I said.

"Of course. But the point is that Reene potentially has all the intel we would ever need, way more than Chorwan could ever have supplied."

"And wouldn't it be handy if we could supply Legion command with his head full of intel versus some low-level criminal?" I added.

Cade grunted. "This is intel I could work with. At least this is progress toward a solution. Good. Legion command didn't expect anything for a few days at any rate, so I could mobilize some things on my end. Maybe get some back up to you two without it being obvious. The Sovereign Worlds seem to have itchy trigger fingers, and I don't need them to shoot first."

"If they did, their aim better be good," Dorn

said darkly. "It would be the last thing they did, regardless."

I smiled despite the circumstances. Those Eridani alphas had the biggest sticks up their asses for protocol, but in battle, they were more ruthless than a Rodinian in battle form. They would show no mercy.

"Anything else I need to know?" Cade asked.

"I think it goes without saying that I will eventually hunt down Isaul Reene and destroy him. Just to give you a heads up, in case Legion command needs you to file paperwork or something."

Cade coughed up a laugh. "Noted, and I expect any of your mate's captors to be barely recognizable smudges on the ground by the time this is all said and done."

"As long as we have an understanding."

"We do," said Cade. "I'm always here to help, Ly."

The comms beeped off and Dorn and I stared at each other in silence.

"We'll need to find the data centers the videos upload to."

I nodded. "Do you think you can hack them?"

"Hack them, harvest them of all their data, and

completely destroy them. I will just need some time."

"We also need to keep Melisande safe."

Dorn smiled. "That's a given. You keep Melisande safe. Leave the hacking and intel to me."

I sighed. "I wonder what we should tell the pimp."

Dorn opened his mouth but was interrupted by a loud knocking on the door. We waited, looking at each other.

The knocking continued. Louder this time.

"Lyova Artox," said the room's computer in a robotic female voice. "Isaul Reene would like to meet with you. Shall I let him in?"

Dorn smirked. "I guess we're going to be going off-script."

I rubbed my eyes. "Dorn, tell me what to say. If I go off-script, I'll rip his head off, and I practically promised Cade I'd be able to deliver this one to Legion command."

"Just be your usual charming self. Tell him you won, so you should've had her."

"That surprisingly was so obvious, I should have come up with it." I sighed and rose to answer the door. "Do I have to let him in? Can't I just kill him, too?"

"We need to find the video center, Ly. Focus on the right things." He tapped his gauntlet, and his Reaper suit bent the light around him so that he was invisible. "I'll follow him out. You stay with Melisande and take care of her."

"Understood." I tapped the door surveillance. "Yes, let him in."

The door slid open and a gray Varon stood, standing next to several guards. One held a tied up Anzel while the others held Chorwan's bloodied and beaten goons.

Anzel's face wasn't looking too good either. He was completely black and blue and his body seeped blood from what looked like multiple wounds, many of which I didn't recall inflicting.

Isaul smiled, stepping lightly into the room. He appeared to be gliding with his black cloaks swaying swiftly around his form, the cloak covering the top of his head. His golden eyes stared shrewdly back at me as if assessing an object.

"Where is she?" Isaul asked, his voice grating, agitating my nerves.

I growled in answer. As if I would tell some bastard where my vulnerable mate was.

"Where is she?" He repeated, enunciating

each word as if there had been something lost in translation.

"I'm here, Master."

I turned at the sound of Melisande's voice. She stood in the doorway connecting into the living quarters, her hair a glorious riot. Her eyes were ringed with dark circles, contrasting with her pale skin. She looked so delicate and fragile wrapped in that bulky blanket.

"Melisande, my darling bird," said Isaul with open arms. "I was so worried."

I curled my hands into fists to keep from pulling Melisande back toward me.

Melisande kept her head low as she dipped into a curtsy. "Master Isaul," she said, as she balanced on her knee.

With one long finger the bastard Reene lifted her chin, turning her from side to side as if he were inspecting her. "You seem more or less whole."

"I am. Thanks to Lyova Artox, Master."

I hated the way she sounded. So docile. Completely devoid of any emotion other than to serve. It was different from the woman in my dreams. From the woman who grabbed me and cried in my arms. Here, she was an empty doll, and

I longed for the moment when I could destroy all who had made her this way.

"Ah, yes, Lyova Artox." Isaul, the bastard, strode past Melisande to stand before me. He looked me up and down. "The great, undefeated champion. You seemed to arrive just in time." He turned to the men tied up, spitting on the ground in front of him. "I should thank you for stopping these idiots," he said, snapping his fingers. "And leaving them for me to punish." He snapped his fingers, and the guards hauled Anzel and Chorwan's men up.

Anzel struggled against his restraints. "No. I am a great gladiator. I didn't do anything!"

Isaul whirled around, grabbing Anzel's jaw with one hand, silencing him with a squeeze. "You conspired with Chorwan without speaking with me. Me!" He shouted in the man's face. "Anyone who wants her," he said, pointing to Melisande, "discusses it with me not with Chorwan, or any other horny bastard who wants her. Me! I am her master. Her legal mate and owner."

Anzel nodded quickly.

Isaul threw him to the guards, wiping his hand on his cloak as if he had touched putrid trash. Anzel whimpered as the guards took him away.

"Now," said Isaul, clapping his hands together. "Where is Chorwan?" Isaul strode back to my mate, touching her hair lightly. "I haven't been able to find him. Or remains of him."

I shrugged. "You won't. I wanted Melisande for myself. I saw her in the VIP box and knew I had to have her." I crossed my arms. "I was annoyed when Anzel was offered her when I defeated him. So, I challenged Chorwan, he lost."

"And his body?"

"Let's just say that he lost really bad." I was aware that Reene was trying to get me to fully admit that I had murdered Chorwan, but there was enough ambiguity there that he would have a hard time trying to blackmail me. Not that it would matter.

Isaul chuckled. "Clever," he said. "It's so wonderful you were able to punish the bastard and return my property. I thank you for that." He wrapped his arm around Melisande's waist and pulled her toward him. "Now we best be on our way. I'm afraid Melisande needs some rest after such an event."

I lunged, grabbing Melisande's arm without thinking. "I would like to have Melisande as my escort for the duration of the tournament."

Isaul stared at me, his eyes narrowing on my hand linked with Melisande's. I doubled down and wrapped an arm around her shoulders. She didn't move away, and the beast inside me roared in triumph.

"Oh?" Isaul looked at Melisande for a moment. "I have many other beautiful women you could choose from."

"I'm sure, and yet I want Melisande."

Isaul shrugged. "Well, you can't have her."

This *motherfucking* bastard. My patience wore thin. "I did return her to you. Untouched. And, healed."

"And I thank you for that." Isaul crossed his arms. "Choose another."

"Master Reene," I held back my growl, but it was difficult. "I really must insist. I did win the match yesterday. And Melisande," I glanced at her, my gaze lingering on her lips, "is extravagantly beautiful."

Isaul glanced between us. His eyes narrowing into tiny little slits. "It would be quite expensive. She is already tired as it is and, not to mention, fragile. She would require extra care."

Extra money, you mean, you insufferable bastard. Instead, I simply said, "I can pay."

"I don't know." Isaul rubbed his chin. "What do you think, Melisande? Could you possibly suffer through another taxing assignment?"

He was goading her. He was testing to see if she would toss herself to me. I watched the way he stood, the way he looked at her. He wanted to see if she wanted me.

The bastard was sneaky.

Melisande looked away from me, dropping her gaze to the floor. "I would do whatever you may ask of me, Master Isaul. Your decision is my wish."

Isaul pursed his lips. "Since you have relieved me of my payor, you must pay for the time he would have spent with her, and then your two days."

As if money had any bearing on me. "Done," I said without hesitation. "Send the invoice to the room."

"I see," his eyes gleamed. "Consider the contract instated."

"If that's the case, then get the fuck out. I don't want to see you until the contract ends."

Isaul Reene was smart and kept his mouth shut. I almost wished he hadn't been. Almost.

With Melisande by my side, I was able to maintain my composure, threadbare as it was.

I watched the bastard leave without so much as a backward glance. I committed every detail about him to memory.

When this was over, I would have my own hunt.

I watched Isaul leave in complete awe. He didn't take me away. He allowed me to stay.

Isaul was up to something.

I was radio silent for so long, I wondered if he scoured the city, perhaps paid Chorwan's suites a visit. That was probably how he had found those other men.

Then, he likely waited for me to open my eyes and give him any hint to where I was.

He had come to take me back to the facility. Or, more likely, off-planet to another location to keep me off-balance. He would be planning something. A back-up plan. He loved money, but he wanted secrets most of all. And I was only too aware of the type of secrets that someone like Lyova could give him.

Especially someone who didn't seem to care about the amount of money he threw around.

I sighed, my energy completely leaving me and my body giving out. Lyova's arms surrounded me, hauling me up close to him. I nestled into his chest and moaned.

"I'm so sorry," I whispered.

"It's fine," said Lyova, pushing my hair back and stroking my face. "You're exhausted. You were drugged and nearly raped."

"Your match," I said, trying valiantly to show that I could stand under my own power. "I should help you prepare for it. What do you need?"

Lyova smiled, making me feel all sorts of fuzzy warm feelings. He was so handsome. The way he stared at me made me feel so loved. It was a look I wanted to keep with me forever.

"How about we start with a bath first," he said, taking my hand and leading me back to his bedroom and through to an ensuite bathroom. The mirrors lit up as we entered. A large tub stood at the center, with a large white stand covered in various jars. I lifted the lids, feeling unusually curious as I found sweetly fragrant oil and bath salts.

"How would you like your bath prepared, Lyova?"

He took my hands in his and pressed them to his lips. "First, you can call me Ly, and second," he pulled my hair to one side, giving him access to place his lips lightly on my neck. I leaned into the touch, my eyes fluttering closed. "Next, why don't I give you a bath, Melisande?"

I paused, not knowing exactly what to say. It would be strange to refuse, since he was now my client, but wouldn't Isaul find it strange? No male had ever asked to bathe me, even as a kink.

"I-I don't know," I turned away, walking a few steps from him and his warmth. I didn't want to turn him down. But I was worried what Isaul would think.

I fucking hated him for intruding, even now when he was not even physically here.

"Or you can bathe yourself, if you'd like?" Lyova sounded earnest, boyish, even. I wished things were different. I wished I could be myself around him. "Whatever you prefer, Melisande."

The way he said my name made my heart race. I didn't want him to leave.

I wanted him to touch me.

I pushed thoughts of Isaul to the side, allowing myself just this once to feel something. To want something for myself. I pulled at the robe covering me.

I heard Lyova's subtle intake of breath as I turned around. A growl of approval vibrated in his chest. His gaze roved over my breasts, my waist, my hips. Many males have seen me without my clothes on. With Lyova, rather than feeling exposed and ashamed, I felt free.

I sauntered toward him until I was mere inches from touching him. He didn't touch me, only looked at me like I was his goddess and he was my loyal servant coming for worship.

"Is this what you wanted?"

"Yes," he breathed, turning on the faucet and allowing the water to run.

I stepped into the tub, setting my head on the rim and waiting for the water to fill. Lyova knelt beside me, softly brushing my hair as the water poured in, warming my chilled body. I listened to the sound, closing my eyes and relishing how gentle Lyova brushed the tangles from my hair. I released a contented sigh as he massaged my scalp, his fingers moving down to my neck and shoulders.

He turned off the water when the liquid sloshed at the top, covering me up to the neck. Grabbing a sponge, he massaged my shoulders, traveling down to my arms in a slow rhythmic pattern. I willed my muscles to relax, trying not to feel self-conscious as he stared down at my naked body.

It worried me, knowing I never wanted this moment to end. Or that in just two short days I would be returning to Isaul.

Or that something terrible could happen to Lyova in that time.

"Relax, Melisande," he whispered in my ear. "It's just you and me here."

I sighed as he kissed my ear.

The sponge dipped into the water, stroking delicate paths in a back and forth rhythm on my stomach. He massaged the skin under my breasts. His knuckles nudged my nipples lightly. I sighed, rolling my head from side to side as he applied more pressure. His knuckles continued to stroke my breasts under the water. My legs parted willingly.

"You are so beautiful, Melisande," Lyova whispered in my ear. "Absolutely beautiful."

He kissed my neck, his teeth grazing the sensitive flesh there. I gave him more access, allowing him to continue kissing the length of me. His hand released the sponge. One hand coming up to stroke my cheek while the other cupped my breast. He played with my nipple, palming it, pinching it.

I arched my back and moaned, the water sloshing around me.

His other hand slid against my stomach, sliding across my body until he found my hand. Lacing his fingers with mine, he led my hand to rest against the juncture of my thighs.

He nipped my ear, nuzzling his nose into my nape. "I want to see you touch yourself." He breathed. "Can I see you, Melisande?"

"Would you like that?" I whispered against his mouth.

He nodded slowly, his eyes on my lips. "Very much. But only if you want to, kitten."

It had been so long since I thought of my own sexual pleasure. And the mere idea that he cared made my eyes prickle. I blinked back the tears and released a shaky breath. Sliding my hand away from his I reached for that little nub, lightly stroking it. I moaned as I felt myself already filling with pleasure, adding more pressure as I circled around it.

He nuzzled my shoulder, his eyes on my hand as I circled around myself, a finger going in and out of my entrance. He kissed my cheek. My lips searched for his, claiming him. He moaned as my tongue tangled with his, my hand pulled at his mane.

I wanted him.

I imagined my fingers were his cock pushing into me. I imagined him rubbing himself against my clit.

"Do you like this?" I gasped.

"Oh, yes," he breathed.

I pushed in another finger, going in and out of me frantically, wishing it was him.

I pulled him forward, trying to tug him into the tub, but he remained rooted in his chair. I wanted him to be deep inside me. I wanted him to fill me up, make me scream his name, make me forget my own. "Lyova," I breathed. "I want you to touch me."

He moaned, sinking his arms into the water and finding my clit. I moaned when he touched me. His lips were on me, his tongue darting inside hungrily. He nipped my lips, sucking on my lower.

I moaned, feeling myself climb higher. Feeling

myself go mad with want as I delved deeper into this fiery, tortuous pleasure.

His fingers replaced mine, one slipping inside easily, followed by a second. His fingers were thicker, longer than mine, reaching areas I couldn't. I thrust against him, his thumb continuing its ministrations.

I gasped as my pleasure climbed higher. A third finger entered me, and I was bearing down against him, meeting each thrust inside me.

I arched my back, crying out his name. My nails dug and clawed against his skin. I thrust against him, water sloshing onto the floor. He moaned, shivering as I screamed his name, my nails digging into him, drawing blood. Pleasure permeated through me as I gasped for breath.

Lyova gazed down at me, filled with hunger. He scooped me up into his arms and stepped into the tub fully clothed. Capturing my lips, he kissed me deeply, spearing my mouth with his skillful tongue. Somehow, he made the water drain away, and the hot jets of the shower pummeled our bodies.

"Let's make sure we've rinsed the soap away," he said in the gentlest voice.

I looked up at him, smiling as he made sure all

of me was suds-free. His hands roamed my body, and I sighed against his touch. He slowly knelt before me and wrapped his arms around my hips. I didn't understand what he was doing until I felt his clever tongue lick along my seam.

I gasped, closing my eyes against the intensity, keeping this all to myself.

He nudged my legs apart, finding my clit and teasing me with gentle licks. The ridges on his tongue hit me just right, and soon I was grinding my hips against his face.

He sank his large fingers inside of me, finding my spot and teasing it even as he lapped at my clit in hypnotic circles.

I unraveled for him, trusting that he would keep me from falling even as I screamed for him.

"There now. All clean." After that declaration, he rose to his feet and kissed me soundly. "Stay right here where it's warm." Lyova stepped out of the shower, clothes dripping wet, and went who knows where.

I couldn't help but giggle. Maybe it was the after effects of a really good orgasm, or maybe it was just him, but I hadn't felt this giddy in a long time. Maybe not ever.

When he returned, I had the dopiest smile on

my face, but I didn't care. I lunged at him and kissed him with wild abandon. Somehow, he managed to turn off the water and wrap me in the fluffy robe that he had brought to me. "There now, much better, I'd say, yes?"

I nodded, preferring to have more of him than words in my mouth.

He pulled me close, propping me up against his body so that I could kiss him at my leisure. I wanted to tell him how much he meant to me. I wanted him... needed him.

I poured all of that into my kiss, into my hands that I buried in his beautiful mane. Every part of me that pressed against him, spoke to my undying wish to be with him from this point forward.

I wanted his hot cock as it pulsed against me. I wanted him to slam me up against the wall and thrust into me. I wanted him now. I nibbled on my bottom lip to keep myself from shoving him into the wall and demanding he do just that.

Instead, I rested my forehead against his, painfully aware that now was not the right time for us. "We should get you ready for your competition."

"Right," he rasped. "The tournament. I'll let

you finish getting ready." With one more hot look, he left me alone in the bathroom.

How was I ever going to survive without him after this?

I SAT IN THE VIP BOX WEARING THE DRESS Lyova bought for me. He had it sent over shortly after he left and I was surprised he had the time to find something so lovely for me to wear. It was either that or his robe.

I was never wearing that white dress ever again.

The garment Lyova chose was beautiful. It was green, which went well with my eyes. The garment had a low back, halting just above my ass with ample view of my cleavage. It clung to my skin like a glove but moved with me. The fabric felt sensuous and I was excited for what he had planned for such a dress.

I sat alone, watching Lyova tear into an opponent, feeling dizzy just from watching him. Every time his sword clanged against his opponent's; I felt his teeth at my neck. Every time he kicked, launching his opponent back, I felt my fingers enter me, my thumb circling around my nub and lighting a fire within me. Every time I heard him growl, I felt his breath at my nape, his whispers at my throat, his fingers teasing my breasts.

"You're so beautiful, Melisande."

I stifled a moan and shifted in my seat, taking a long sip from the wine, hoping it would dull this insatiable longing.

I saw movement out of the corner of my eye and turned, watching Isaul push through the narrow paths, making a poor woman and her husband miss Lyova throwing his opponent across the arena. The crowd jeered, stomping their feet and Isaul received a dark glare from the couple.

"That's another win for Lyova Artox!" Shouted the robot, showing a holographic image of the opponent tapping the ground.

Lyova raised his hands, winking at me for a moment before doing several backflips through the arena. The crowd cheered louder.

"Melisande," came Isaul's grating voice.

I sighed as he took his seat next to mine,

refusing to acknowledge him. My client was Lyova and I was supposed to pay attention to his match. It would be rude if I ignored him during an important tournament, right?

I think it would.

Isaul didn't need my attention all the time.

"Introducing Lynell Taus!" Shouted the announcer. I grimaced as I watched a beastly looking Varon enter the arena, dressed in all black lined in spikes. He shrieked, flexing his muscles before lunging toward Lyova.

Lyova side stepped and swiped at Lynell's legs, making him flip and land on his back. He hovered over Lynell, punching him in the face until he tapped the ground three times. Lyova raised his arms in victory and paraded himself around the arena as victor.

"Lyova Artox wins again!"

He was absolutely magnificent.

"I must applaud you on attracting Lyova's attention," said Isaul, leaning over his chair to whisper his words in my ear.

He didn't sound applauding. He sounded coy. As if he were up to something. I kept my attention on Lyova, standing and applauding as he ran past me, scowling at Isaul before pouncing into the air.

The crowd erupted into a strew of cheers.

When I sat, Isaul was holding out something. A tablet, displaying my debt and my accounts. My eyes widened on the numbers. My heart was swelling with joy, but I couldn't show it. I mustn't. Or else Isaul would do something.

He always knew how to hurt me.

"Introducing..." the announcer called, but I was no longer interested in the match, but in the numbers in front of me.

I blinked. The numbers still stared back at me. I waited for him to do something. To say something. To take it all away.

But he only sat, holding out the screen.

6,000,000/5,133,900 it read.

I had 6,000,000 credits.

I could pay my debt.

I could finally be free.

Isaul chuckled. "He paid quite well. Even gave you a substantial tip." I glanced at Isaul, watching him lick his lips. "It's enough to pay for your freedom."

"Yes," I breathed, touching the screen lightly. "It is."

"However, it was quite expensive to get you here," Isaul said, nodding and deducting the numbers. "And with the food and that extravagant white dress…" I watched the numbers lowering.

5,000,000…

"Your accommodation was quite an expense…"

3,555,000…

"Ah, yes, and the language nanotechnology," he sneered. "Quite an expense indeed."

80,050.

That was what I was left with.

I gazed back at the numbers with glistening eyes. I didn't want to cry, especially in front of Isaul, but I still felt a tear slide down my cheek.

He swiped at it with a long finger, putting it between his lips to taste. I grimaced, disgusted and horrified at the same time. I couldn't even concentrate on the next match.

"You will always be mine, Melisande," he whispered, tucking a stray strand behind my ear. I turned away from him, turning my gaze back on the match. I refused to look at him as I focused on Lyova, twirling his sword. "Even if someone like Lyova Artox does pay well and tip high, you will still always belong to me."

I didn't respond.

I watched Lyova pounce, swiping his sword against his opponent's shield before dodging a swipe at his side. He rolled, dodging another strike before jumping into a standing position and slashing his opponent's leg.

"I am the only one you have, Melisande," Isaul whispered in my ear. "The only one who will care for you. The only one who will ensure your safety. You have no one else, but me. If you truly know what's best for you, you will get that through your thick skull. The sooner the better."

I imagined Lyova's opponent to be Isaul. I imagined his tall, thin form holding up the shield, hiding behind it as Lyova ripped it from his hands and broke it into pieces over his knee. I imagined Lyova grabbing him by the throat and tossing him across the arena. Imagined him punching his sneering gray face into the ground until it was unrecognizable.

I imagined Lyova turning to me, holding out his hand and kissing me in the arena over Isaul's limp form.

I blinked.

But it wasn't Isaul's body out in the arena, being carted away in a stretcher. Isaul was sitting next to me, expecting some sort of response.

And at the end of the day, I knew he was right.

I knew I would never be free of him.

That I would be his until the day I died.

"Melisande," Isaul patted my hand. It took everything within me not to flinch from his touch. Where Lyova was warm, he was cold, clammy. "It pains me to see you like this."

Yeah, right.

"It's actually a good thing you are with Lyova Artox. He comes from nobility, you know?"

I shook my head. "I didn't know," I said calmly. Sadly, I barely knew him and it wasn't like I could get to know him more with Isaul watching me.

"It would be nice if you could find something on him," his fingers crawled up my arm, straightening my strap. "If you find some dirt on him, I could give you those pretty rooms above the clouds. Wouldn't that be nice?"

Ah, so that cat is finally out of the bag. Isaul wanted dirt. I should have known.

"Do you think you can help me out, Melisande?" Isaul's hand ran up and down the length of my arm. I wanted to smack his fingers away, but the sooner he left the better.

I turned to him, smiling sweetly as I did with all my clients. "Of course, Master."

I DODGED AROUND THE OTHER FIGHTER AS THE crowd cheered my name.

I barely heard them. All I could hear was how Melisande cried out as I held her in the bath. As I tasted her in the shower. I whirled around, twirling my sword before swiping forward and nicking my opponent.

Everything reminded me of her. Her mouth against my neck, her hands tugging my mane. Even the claw marks on my arm made my cock hard.

Fuck. I wanted to be inside her, claiming her, marking her as my mate, and bonding with her forever. I wanted to hear her screaming my name over and over again until it was the only word she knew. I wanted to bury myself inside her, become one with her, until her scent suffocated me.

I barely had time to jump over the sword aimed for my head, catching sight of Melisande sitting in the dress I chose for her. I knew the color would bring out her eyes. It hugged her curves in just the right way.

And as beautiful as she was in it, I couldn't wait to get her out of the garment.

But why was Isaul sitting next to her? I made it clear that I didn't want to see his face until after the contract was done. He was leaning over his chair, whispering something into Melisande's ear. In his hand was a tablet. Was he showing her something?

I twirled my sword, but my sight wasn't on my opponent, what's-his-face, but on Isaul. I swiped my sword, hitting my opponent's, the sound ringing throughout the arena. I looked past my challenger's gaze and watched Isaul's smirk. Melisande was still staring at the tablet. Just what was she looking at?

Fuck this. Time to wrap up this fight. I grabbed my challenger by his armor and pulled him closer, punching him in the face and kicking him backwards.

I slammed my sword down, but my opponent

kicked out, pushing me back. I stumbled backward for a moment, catching my balance as he stood. He swiped his sword at my stomach, missing by a hair. I blocked his next strike before flipping backwards several times to gain distance.

All right, Ly. You got a match to win. Melisande is safe and sound and you can cheer her up after you win this tournament.

With any luck, Dorn found the evil video center and had it destroyed before dinner.

My opponent cried out, charging forward with his sword. I pounced, landing behind him. I whirled around and slammed my sword against his. I slashed blow against blow on my opponent, the swords ringing. I swiped again, shattering his sword into pieces.

He punched at me, but before it could land, I caught his arm, breaking it over my shoulder. He screamed as I flipped him over, knocking his head against the ground. My beast threatened to rise, rage and fury warring within me as I saw this tournament as an obstacle that was keeping me from claiming my mate as I ought to.

The hovering robot flew forward as he laid there, not moving. The robot counted down the time, the crowd joining in. "Lyova Artox wins!"

The crowd erupted into cheers as holographic flowers fell from the sky, raining down around me. Everyone around me stood, clapping and shouting my name.

I whirled around, seeing Melisande smiling, shouting my name.

My inner beast calmed, the red rage abating from my vision as I locked eyes with her. I inhaled deeply, smelling her scent, feeling her around me.

My beautiful, fiery mate. She made me whole.

.

I STOOD IN FRONT OF THE MIRROR, straightening my suit jacket and button down shirt. My eyes glanced toward the closed door of Melisande's room. There was another winner's circle tonight and she was attending as my date. I still couldn't believe that she was here. With me. If only Isaul wasn't watching our every move, I would make her my mate tonight.

The faint beep of comms interrupted my thoughts. I quickly answered, secretly hoping that Dorn found where Isaul saved his blackmail videos and somehow hacked the data on his own. "Did you find anything?"

"No. That Varon is always surrounded by guards," came Dorn's voice.

Damned coward. Isaul Reene played the game of being the big, bad boss, but in the end he was just a coward. "He was easy to spot and easy to follow. I found the video controls he keeps. It's on the bottom floor of this building. Pretty dark down here, I've gotta say."

Fuck yes. Finally, something was going right.

"Unfortunately, it, too, is heavily guarded."

I groaned and rubbed my temples. Of course, it was. "We don't have much time, Dorn."

"I know, but I cannot get in now. I'll set up surveillance and see if there are any gaps in the guard changes. Or if there is any other way to get in and out quickly."

The door opened and Melisande stood in the entrance, wearing a beautiful glittering black dress. "Keep me updated." I turned off comms.

"You are beautiful," I said, the image of her completely taking my breath away. I strode toward her, unable to stop myself from cupping her cheek. I touched my forehead to hers, breathing her scent in and allowing it to wash away my worries.

Heat flushed her cheeks, making her appear even more lovely. "Thank you," she whispered, nuzzling her nose against mine.

I took her hand, wrapping it around my arm. My eyes never left her. I couldn't possibly stop looking at her. Nothing else seemed to matter.

I escorted her down the long hallway toward the Grand Hall, trying to find anything to say to her, but finding everything I came up with inadequate.

"You were amazing today," she said softly.

"You think?" I cringed inwardly at how awkward I sounded. Like an untested juvenile.

However, thinking of the fight today brought my thoughts to Isaul and his little visit. I ground my teeth, imagining all the terrible things the bastard said to her. I didn't want to risk Isaul over-hearing our conversation or tip our hand that we know about his movements. Or let on that I noticed that she had disappeared for a couple hours after the match.

The doors opened and the Grand Hall's deco-ration had changed from twinkling stars to a whim-sical moonlit night with holographic water splashing into the hall and a great moon lighting the dance floor. Lanterns hovered above with twin-kling bulbs glistening around the banquet tables, piled high with food. Servants passed by, carrying trays of wine and I quickly grabbed two glasses, handing one to Melisande.

"I'm glad you enjoyed the fight," I said, not knowing what more to say. Knowing Isaul was watching didn't help with the matter. "I look forward to the final match tomorrow."

"Are you nervous?" She asked, taking a sip of the wine. Her lush lips parted in a tender smile. Star's blazes, did I want her.

"Nervous?" I straightened my spine and flexed my muscles, striking a silly pose that I knew would make her laugh. I was rewarded by her joyous giggles. "Not at all. I know I'll win."

"Ah, so you're a fortune-teller now?" Melisande said.

I shrugged. "I've done this long enough."

She leaned in close, her scent fogging my senses. I inhaled deeply, closing my eyes and savoring her proximity. "I'll be rooting for you, Ly," she whispered in my ear.

I growled pulling her close, wanting to shove her against the wall and capture those seductive lips of hers. My cock grew thick and hard, and her rubbing herself against me was slowly making me lose my mind. She nipped my ear lightly, before pushing herself away.

"Later," she said. With that one word, filled with promise, I followed her across the hall to the tables, watching the way the dress swished around her legs and hugged her ass in the most perfect way.

Melisande grabbed a plate of grapes, taking one to pop inside my mouth. I swallowed the grape whole, sucking on her fingers lightly and watching her eyes dilate as they gazed back at me. I snatched the plate from her hands and ushered her toward a sofa near the wall.

Melisande sat in the cushions waiting for me and I sat on the armrest, leaning over as I fed her, watching as she took each delectable bite. Watching her teeth break the skin and wishing it was mine. Watching her tongue lick the juices and imagining that tongue on my cock. She watched me as she ate, not taking her gaze away from me for a single moment.

"Lyova Artox!" Came a familiar call, breaking my trance.

I turned, seeing Isaul striding toward us with his arms out as if the bastard would hug me. If he touched me, I didn't think I could possibly hold back. I would probably pound his face in. What a lovely image that would make.

I didn't bother to move, to take his hand, to stand or do anything to register our familiarity. Isaul dropped his arms awkwardly, glancing back and forth between us before landing his narrowed eyes on Melisande. Instantly, she bounded up from the sofa and took the plate from my hands.

"Let me serve you," she said in an emotionless tone, as if Melisande had completely left the building and was replaced by a sex robot.

I opened my mouth, about to tell her to relax and Isaul to fuck off when that bastard clapped me on the shoulder.

"Congratulations on your win, Lyova Artox," said Isaul, leaning in close and smiling as if we were close friends. "I'm sure the Rodinian nobility are quite proud of your outstanding attributes."

I raised an eyebrow. The Rodinians didn't really stand on ceremony. The strong served and protected the weak. In that respect, yes, they were proud. "Sure," I said, scowling back at the pimp. "And I thought I wouldn't have to see your face."

"I was wondering if I could have a moment of your time?"

"Sure," I answered instead. I reached for Melisande's hand, giving it a gentle squeeze, but stopped when I saw Isaul's gaze narrow on the small affection.

Fuck.

"Stay here," I ordered, sounding gruffer than need be, but I didn't need Isaul questioning our connection. Fate-mates were a legend in my culture, worshiped and sacred. I had no clue how much the Varons knew of our love for our mates.

I followed Isaul into an alcove, fighting the need to look back and make sure Melisande was all right; that no one was bothering her. Even though she seemed fine since her near assault it didn't mean that she was fine.

"I'm sure you've noticed how traumatized and worn down Melisande has been."

She's stronger than you think, you wormy little asshole. I didn't bother answering. I straightened my shoulders and my head, hoping I seemed even larger and more dangerous than before as I towered over him. Isaul shuffled from side to side, glancing around briefly before leaning forward.

"Usually, sexual relations are included in the price, however I am quite concerned about Melisande's mental state. Especially after what happened to her."

I scowled. You don't care at all, you fucking little twat. All you want is more money.

"I'm sure, after such an amazing battle today, you would love to have some... release," Isaul smirked and I fought back the need to grab him by his puny little throat. "I could give you a discount since you are the great, undefeated gladiator. However, it would depend on what exactly you would like to do."

I raised an eyebrow, my curiosity taking hold. I told myself not to ask; that it would only upset me knowing what this monster had been making her do, but still, I felt the words leave my stupid mouth, "What exactly have you been making Melisande do?"

Isaul's smile widened, his eyes going crazed. "Making her? Why, she's a business woman! A khosa is in charge of her own way of entertainment, whatever that might be."

I fought back the anger rising inside of me. My beast raged against my control as this slimy bastard spoke of our mate. Glancing at Melisande; sweet, beautiful Melisande and imagining her forced into doing all these things with different clients.

I clenched my jaw, watching her on the sofa as she drank her wine, running her fingers through her hair. She glanced back at me for a moment, her lips twitching into a soft, shy smile, before she quickly looked away.

She wasn't broken. She was strong. She was a survivor.

She was all mine, and I was getting her out of this mess.

"I don't think I will be needing any of those services," I said, already walking away from Isaul and back to my mate. Melisande was mine. I would never pressure her into anything she didn't want to do. I wasn't going to discuss my sexual wants and needs with a man I despised. When Melisande was ready, I would be the one to service her and care for her sexual needs.

All I wanted right now was to pleasure her. Hear her scream my name again. Mark my body with her nails. But only on her terms and when she was ready.

Isaul caught my hand and I shook him off. "Didn't I say that I had no wish to see your face until the end of the contract?" I growled, scowling down at him and watching him shrink.

In his hunched form, he still had the audacity to smirk. "Have it your way," he hissed. "However,

I have my ways of finding out if she pleasures you without paying."

"I'm sure you do."

Isaul shrugged. "Fine. Have it your way. Remember, she is my legal mate. She belongs to me, mind, body, and soul."

I watched Isaul slink back into the shadows, ensuring he actually left the hall rather than stalk my mate. I turned back, wanting to pull her into my arms and never let her go.

I dipped into a shadowed alcove and looking around to ensure no one was in eavesdropping distance and brought up Dorn on comms. "Please tell me you found something."

"Night guard leaves every night to have sex with a server."

Star's blazes, progress. "How long should we have?"

"Twenty minutes."

"Is that enough time?"

"Should be."

"When do they meet?"

Dorn chuckled. "You have two hours, Ly. Make them count. Over and out." He cut comms.

There were times that I really appreciated

Dorn's direct, no-nonsense manner. Times like now.

I turned off comms, watching Melisande in the distance.

Soon, she would be all mine. Mind, body, and soul.

I FELT FOR THE VIAL IN MY DRESS POCKETS AS I walked next to Lyova back to his quarters. I had meant to meet Lyova after the match, but after listening to some talk about the black market from the other servants and escorts, I'd decided to hell with Isaul. I was going to do something for myself.

I'd left, taking myself down to the dreary streets below in search of something that would allow me to be with Lyova.

After having Isaul lingering over my shoulder these past few years, I didn't want him taking any part of my time with Lyova. Especially this time. I wanted Ly. I wanted him more than I've ever wanted anything for myself.

Touching the vial now, I remembered walking

down the dripping streets, and recalled how quiet it was compared to the arena above. The escorts had said there was a very skilled doctor in the black market, lingering under the neon blue tower with the tournament advertisement.

He had a no-nonsense demeanor of a war veteran. Someone who had seen too much to be fazed by anything. He had taken a vial out of his desk drawer without hesitation and handed it to me. "This will last for approximately an hour."

"Only an hour?"

"More will cost. The more common this is, the more certain handlers will wonder why their tech is malfunctioning. Only one dosage. Two could kill you. But one is enough. Take it when you're ready and it will seem as if you went to sleep."

He held the vial out to me. I hesitated. "Will it hurt me?"

"Not at all."

I reached for it, but the doctor stepped back. "Payment first."

I held out my chip, not bothering to ask how much it would be. It didn't matter. I would never be free. I never wanted anything more for in my life. All that mattered was this one moment with Ly.

Now, watching Lyova, I'm so happy I didn't allow my fear to stop me. We could be together for this hour without Isaul watching.

I watched Ly unlock the door, watching him stride inside, pulling off his suit jacket. "Would you like something to drink?" He asked, not bothering to turn around.

I pulled out the vial, uncorking it and downed the bitter tasting concoction. Lyova was still busying himself with the refrigerator as I pulled the straps down from my dress, feeling the fabric slide against my skin as it slipped to a heap on the floor.

I had been waiting for this moment since I left the black market. I wore nothing under the dress; only my stiletto black heels. I waited for Ly to turn around and when he did, he dropped the glasses. As they shattered on the floor, I strode toward him, pressing a hand against his chest and pinning him against the wall behind him.

"Wait," his voice was hoarse, he licked his lips, his hands skimming against my skin.

I eased into him, lifting my thigh against his hip. My lips pressed against his, tasting him. My tongue dipped inside, swallowing his moan while my hands undid the buttons of his dress shirt.

"Wait," Lyova said against my lips. He tried to push me away, but I swallowed each of his "waits" with my kisses, feeling his cock growing hard against me. I rubbed my clit against it, swallowing another of his moans.

"Enough of this 'wait,'" I whispered against his lips, tugging on his lower with my teeth. "We only have an hour."

He groaned, leaning his head against my shoulder as he rubbed his cock against me. "We can't do this. Isaul is watching," he paused, lifting his head and gazing down on me, "What do you mean we only have an hour?"

"Isaul isn't watching," I breathed.

His hands were already on my hips, picking me up and taking me to his bed. My legs wrapped around him. "What do you mean?" He said between kisses on my neck, his hand cupping my ass. I arched against him.

"I took something to block out the surveillance," I gasped.

He laid me gently down on the bed, throwing off his suit jacket and then pulling off his shirt. "How?" He gasped, grabbing my breast, pinching my nipple between his knuckles.

I groaned as I reached for his belt, undoing and

pulling his pants down quickly. "Enough questions," I whispered before capturing his mouth for
another searing kiss.

I reached for his cock, palming against the stiff-
ness and feeling him grow in length. He was huge.
Just like in my dreams. And I had him all to
myself.

Lyova grabbed my hands, pinning them down
at my side. His mouth pressed hot kisses into my
neck, drawing a path down to my breasts. He
nipped at my nipples and instinctively I tightened
my thighs around him. My clit rubbed against his
cock, already free from his underwear and leaking
pre-cum on my stomach.

I ran a hand down the length of my body, slipping my fingers inside my hot, slick cunt, already
wetting the comforter. I slipped a finger inside as
Lyova sucked on my breasts, his hot tongue traveling around one as his knuckles pinched and
pulled the other.

Lyova moaned against me. "You feel so good."
His breath sent tingles down my breasts to my core.

He pulled my fingers away from me, sucking
my slick from one. "You taste amazing," he whispered, kissing my palm. He kissed a path down my
arm before changing direction, his tongue traveling

around my slick clit and circling around the little nub of pleasure.

He sucked on me, grazing his teeth against it lightly as he inserted one finger deep inside me. His finger was long and thick and felt so good. His mouth released me and I whimpered, wanting more. He gazed up at me, his face flushed, his eyes drunk with sex. His thumb rubbed me and he dipped his head to graze his teeth against my thigh, inserting another finger inside.

I moaned, arching as I felt him push and rub against my insides, preparing me for his large cock. I ground against his fingers, but it wasn't enough.

I needed more.

"Wait," I gasped as he inserted another finger inside me.

Lyova immediately stopped, lifting his head and staring at me like a lost puppy, waiting for his master's next command. "What's wrong?" He whispered, his fingers leaving me. He crawled up to me, kissing each side of my face and my nose. "Did I hurt you?"

I sat up in the bed and rolled him over, pressing him into the cushions. I felt the base of his dick against my ass, bobbing against my skin. I straddled his hips, kissing a path seductively down his chest, sucking his nipple then biting it. He hissed and his hands tightened around me.

I smirked. "I want to taste you," I whispered, sucking a path down his stomach until I reached his hard, well-endowed cock.

I stared at it, trying to imagine his length pounding into me. There was no way he was going to fit inside me. Not without a lot of prep work, that was for sure. I pursed my lips, suddenly feeling very aware that we had limited time. I really wanted to have him inside me.

But how?

"It's okay," Lyova said, trying to pull me back to him. "We don't have to do anything. This is enough for me."

This was definitely not enough for me. "Hush now," I said, as I placed a kiss on his tip. His eyes rolled to the back of his head and he groaned when I licked his slit. I thrilled when he gasped as I took his tip into my mouth, tasting him. I tried to take him deeper, my tongue circling around the ribbed flesh.

I couldn't take him as deep as I wanted to. Maybe one day, I could work up to it. Instead, I gripped the base of him as I worked his tip. He grew impossibly hard and I ached to have him inside of me.

"I want all of this inside of me."

"Yes," he hissed, drawing out the word. "I want to be inside of your tight, wet pussy."

I crawled up the length of him, rubbing my clit against his tip. "Then, fuck me, Ly," I whispered in his ear. "I want to feel you inside me."

Lyova rolled me over and pulled my legs around his hips. His thumb rubbed my clit as he looked down on me. "I'll be gentle," he whispered before inserting his tip inside me.

I groaned at the sensation of him going inside me coupled with his slow movements on my nub. He waited for me to get used to his girth, pushing deeper and deeper with each slow, dragging stroke. "More," I groaned.

Lyova moved slowly, stopping when I hissed and continuing when I moaned. I felt myself stretch and pulse around him, felt my body taking him in. My moans grew louder as he entered me fully, bottoming out. The ridges along the base of his cock rubbed deliciously against my clit.

He pressed down against me, watching me as pleasure racked through my body. "Are you all right?"

I nodded, my legs squeezing around his hips. I arched against him, needing the friction. He was so deep inside me. My body clenched around him and something within me snapped, desperately needing him to move.

"Ly," I whimpered, scrambling to get closer to him. "Ly, for fuck's sake," I moaned, my body moving against him. I couldn't complete whatever thought had come to mind.

Lyova thrust into me slowly, methodically, finding a slow rhythm that was not enough.

I pushed against him. I was in no mood for gentle. Not right now. I pounded against him feverishly. My hands clenched the headboard behind him while the other tried to gain balance on his chest. I felt him meet my thrusts, his breath coming out as pants.

"Fuck," he groaned, dragging the word out as long as possible. "Star's blazes, you're so hot."

He rolled, pinning me to the bed. Pulling my hips back, he sank into me from behind. His hand grabbed the nape of my neck and I hissed pleasure through my teeth. "You like that, kitten?"

I had no words, only primal grunts and noises. I arched my back so he could thrust deeper. His body slid into mine with wanton smacks that made me blush. I'd never felt so wild, so free.

His fingers tangled into my hair, pulling until I was taut as a bowstring. He angled down so he could capture my lips, never breaking his rhythm. "More," he growled against me.

Lyova flipped me over, practically folding me in two as he slammed into me. My ankles were on his shoulder, meeting each thrust.

He grabbed my legs, thrusting them outwards and I screamed as the new angle allowed for him to move deeper inside me. He angled us so I could watch his cock thrusting in and out of me, my legs splayed wide.

"Come for me," he breathed against my lips.

My body bowed in surrender, my nails digging into his shoulders. I screamed his name with wild abandon, pouring every ounce of desperate need I had for him with every breath.

Lyova grew before my eyes, his body becoming larger, his face hardening, becoming more animalistic. His body tensed over me, as if he held back a storm. His shoulders bunched as if boulders moved beneath his skin. His claws tore into the bed, shredding cloth. Fangs grew prominent, even as he clenched his jaws, the corded muscles of his neck showing the strain of controlling his feral beast.

The base of his cock grew larger, stretching my entrance. I'd heard of knotting before but had never experienced it. He gave one mighty thrust and seated his knot inside of me as he came with a shattering roar. Hot jets of fluid splashed inside of me as my muscles squeezed against him.

Breathless, he rasped out my name like a prayer as he rained kisses on my face, wherever he could reach. He was still so much larger than he had been. Large enough that he could hurt me, but he didn't. He turned us over so that he lay on his back, while I was splayed over him, our bodies still fused together.

I gasped, unable to do anything other than lay here for his pleasure. I rested my head against his chest, listening to his heart beating like war drums. His fingers played through my hair. His gentle purr relaxing me, lulling me into a deeper peace than I could remember.

I didn't want to think about how tomorrow was our last day.

I STROKED MELISANDE'S HAIR, KNOWING THE time to leave was arriving. The soft sounds of her breathing told of her sleeping and I didn't want to disrupt her. She was so beautiful. I didn't want to leave her but knew as soon as this was done and over with, I could take her back to the prowler and fly her far away from this place.

Far away from Isaul.

I wondered briefly if the asshole had a GPS tracking device on her, but if he did it wouldn't matter as soon as we returned to Legion. There's no way Isaul could infiltrate the Reapers.

That is, unless he had a death wish.

I sighed, looking at the time. Gently, I moved her head from my chest to the pillows, wrapping her arm around the comforter and pulling my body from the bed. I watched her sleeping soundly, her scent filling the room and making me dizzy.

I felt the pull of bonding when we were together; she must have felt the same way. She must have so many questions but wouldn't want to ask any of them because of those damned surveillance bots inside of her.

Star's blazes, how I wanted to claim her as my mate. Be bonded so that she would never have a doubt about her worth. And we would bond. There wasn't a doubt in my mind that she would choose me. Once I got her away from Isaul, she would be able to choose me—choose us—of her own free will. Until then, I would enjoy winning her over.

I slipped into my Reaper suit. It was like an extension of myself, familiar and I quickly dressed in my black uniform, grabbing a blaster and stuffing it into my utility belt. There was a knock on my door and I answered it, seeing Dorn waiting on the other side. I took one last glance at Melisande before closing the door behind me and following Dorn down the dimly lit hallway.

"It's not too far away," said Dorn, walking quickly and lightly, not making any noise.

"Are you sure we'll have enough time?"

Dorn leaned against the wall, peaking around the corner before tiptoeing across the hall and through a dark kitchen. "We should," he whispered. "It's not like I'm trying to hack anything."

"Would that take longer?"

"Much longer."

I sighed, pulling at my mane. Nerves grabbed hold of me and filled me with images of Melisande being grabbed and taken away in the middle of the night. Something crawled through me, urging me to return to her side.

I took a deep breath, leaning against the wall as Dorn checked the hallways once again.

Ly, once this is done, you can be with Melisande forever, I told myself. *Just focus on something other than your cock for once.*

Dorn took off down the hallway and I followed him, keeping my head low until we were outside in the night air. The wind blew around us, whipping my mane back and forth as I followed Dorn toward a platform. He typed in the coordinates while straps wrapped around our bodies, keeping us in place.

I watched the arena disappear as the platform took us lower and lower into the city. I had never been so low in this place. I covered my face, smelling rot and something else.

"Where are you taking me, Dorn?" I groaned, trying to get away from the smell.

Dorn shrugged. "To the bottom." He sighed. "Unfortunately, the poor are not well cared for in places like these. Just try to keep quiet."

The platform landed and I followed Dorn around the building to a door. He opened it swiftly and tiptoed inside. I took a moment to gaze at the pristine white walls, and the beautiful golden, candelabras.

"Wow," I breathed. "Isaul really knows how to decorate."

Dorn shushed me and I rolled my eyes, following him into another hallway with a tall, stocky Varon standing outside it. He was dressed in a fancy suit that barely fit over his muscles.

"I thought you said he would be gone," I grumbled, already pulling out my blaster.

Dorn waved his hand. "The servant should be coming," Dorn stopped, pointing toward a Varon female with long black hair wearing a tight black dress that barely covered her ass and breasts. "There she is."

I peeked around the corner, watching as she strutted past the Varon, grabbing his tie and dragging him behind her. When they disappeared around the corner, Dorn ran lightly down the hallway, throwing the door open and turning on the lights.

I clicked the door shut and leaned against it. "Well, that was easy." I smirked, about to say something else when I paused, staring up at the videos showing everything Melisande had seen.

"Remember," called Dorn, attaching some tech to the computer. "Twenty minutes." He typed at the screen, pulling down a green visor over his eyes.

"Is that for me, or for you?" I called, not taking my eyes off the videos.

Dorn made a face. "Just stand there and keep watch."

I leaned my head against the door, unable to tear my gaze away from all the video screens. There were twelve in total, replaying particular moments of the day.

There was a yellow haired man in the streets on one screen in the far right. He smiled at her, his eyes going up and down the length of her. He handed her a vial, paying with her card. The numbers went quickly down until all that was in her account was a measly five hundred credits.

Is that where she bought the concoction? What the fuck had she been thinking? She could have been attacked.

"I am the only one you have, Melisande," I jumped hearing Isaul's voice.

For a moment I thought he was behind us, but then remembered the door was behind me. I turned to the middle screen, seeing Isaul's disgusting grey face.

"The only one who will care for you. The only one who will ensure your safety. You have no one else, but me. If you truly know what's best for you, you will get that through your thick skull. The sooner the better."

My hands fisted at my side, watching him next to her, remembering the tears slipping from her eyes. "You have me," I muttered at the screen. "You have me, Melisande. Don't listen to anything that bastard has to say to you."

There was a snap of electricity and then the screens turned black. Dorn popped his head out from behind the computer, striding over and smiling. A smiling Dorn was a scary Dorn.

"What made you so happy?" I asked, watching him.

"I hacked it, stripped it, mined it for all its data. Basically, it's being uploaded to Cade and Legion command."

My heart leaped, not daring to hope that we could be done with this assignment so soon. "And?"

"Oh, and to ensure its inability for use in the future, I may have strapped some detonators to it, so we should go now."

The door was thrown open and two very stocky, well-muscled Varons entered.

I scowled at Dorn. "I thought you said we had twenty minutes?"

Dorn shrugged. "We did."

I groaned, rubbing my face until I heard the countdown behind me. "10, 9, 8—"

"What the fuck, Dorn?"

"Run fast," he called back to me.

I was hot on his trail. He slipped past the guards and I followed his path. Dorn ducked and kicked a guard back into the control room, slamming and holding the door shut. I punched my guard in the balls, watching as he slowly crouched down to the floor, his arm still stuck in the wall.

There was a huge boom behind the door and I stared at Dorn as a siren went off. The guard from before stumbled into the hallway, zipping his fly. The servant girl followed after him for a moment until her eyes landed on us.

"What the—" she shouted.

The guard roared, charging forward and grabbing his blaster. I grabbed Dorn and shoved him forward, running as fast as possible as the guard shot at us. The lighting in the hallway went from pristine white, to a crimson red and the sirens grew louder.

We turned, running down another hallway, but were immediately stopped by three guards running toward us, all wearing the same uniform.

"Shit!" Dorn shouted, his nails lengthening. He pounced, dodging several shots and landing on one of the guards, tearing into his shoulder.

I dodged the bullets, kicking at the walls until I was flipping over the guards. I landed on one's face, hearing his nose snap under my boot. I kicked off him, grabbing another by the neck and throwing him over my shoulder.

More of Isaul's goons ran into the hallway. There were so many. I didn't worry about the numbers.

Until one of them hit us with massive tranqs.
"What the hell?"

When Dorn would have shifted, he gripped his
head with a massive roar, as if he had been kicked
by an invisible soldier.

"Dorn!" I shouted, watching as several guards
overpowered him by sheer weight.

That was when I realized the rage and dark
fury that was a constant battle within me was
eerily quiet. It was as if a piece of myself was
numb.

My beast.

I stared at the massive tranqs that fell from my
body. Somehow, whatever they shot into us quieted
our beast.

I struggled against the men surrounding me. I
would not give up. Melisande needed me.

We were so close. We were so close to being
together.

I roared, pulling at my arm with two guards
holding me back. I ripped myself from their hold
on me and ran back toward the other guard, sliding
and kicking his legs out from under him, but he
was too fast. He grabbed my leg, flipping me
around and slamming me down on the floor.

I tried to roll over as he straddled my legs. My

fist went for his face, but he caught it, pinning it to the ground before he head butted me. I tried to struggle, but he head butted me again.

I blinked. "Get the fuck up, Ly," I growled to myself, seeing red.

I roared, feeling a surge of strength coming to me in weak sputters. It wasn't nullified completely, but I was still not the same. I pulled my arm from my attacker's grip and slashed through his palms, hearing him scream, but not quite seeing. I stood but was quickly slammed into the wall by two men. The other punched me in the face.

I struggled against my restraints. I kicked out from under me, but the Varon was punching me in the face over and over again. Blood ran from my nose and I hung my head, unable to move anymore. I looked over my assailant's shoulder, finding Dorn's limp form on the floor.

I felt my knees hit the ground, felt something wrap around my neck before I fell, unable to get myself back up. I spat blood as I tried to crawl away. The men around me chuckled. Something had my leg. Another stepped on my hand. Another kicked me in the face.

I groaned. "Get up," I told myself, but my head was already resting against the bloodied carpet.

Think of Melisande, I told myself, imagining her head on my chest, smiling up at me as her fingers stroked my mane.

"Melisande," I groaned, my eyes closing. She was going to be so worried. "Melisande."

SOMEONE WAS SHAKING ME. FOR A MOMENT I thought it was just a dream, but there was too much pressure on my shoulder for it to be a simple dream. Quickly, I opened my eyes, biting back a scream when I saw Isaul leaning over me, watching me with those narrow yellow eyes. His tongue darted over his lips, resembling a snake about to strike.

"Wakey-wakey, sweetheart." His sing-song voice belied a simmering anger. Though his mouth turned up in a mockery of a smile, his eyes shone with glittering malice.

A chill came over me, and I grabbed the sheets, covering myself. It didn't matter if Isaul had seen me naked before. He wasn't going to see me now.

Something was very wrong. Lyova would never let that man come anywhere near me in his presence. I swallowed down my emotions, letting them simmer behind my practiced mask. I wouldn't let him goad me into saying or doing something that would give anything away.

"Where's Lyova?" I asked, tightening the blanket around my body as I scowled at his guards.

Isaul tossed my dress onto the bed. "Get dressed."

I stared at him, waiting for more instruction or at least an explanation, but he just stood there, expectantly. Dread filled my heart. Was my commission over already? Did he somehow manage to make Ly finish the contract early? "Of course," I said, as if something like this happened all the time. "Has something happened?"

I took pains to keep my voice neutral, but it was hard when Isaul was in one of his moods. On a normal day, he was passively cruel. In a temper, he was sadistic.

Isaul's smile widened. "You'll find out soon, sweetheart. Off you get." He gestured toward the powder room.

I took the out. It took every ounce of strength inside of me not to run, especially when I could feel the lecherous gazes of Isaul's bodyguards on me. Though I felt like prey once more, I drew upon the courage that Ly always showed to the world. His confidence.

Where was he? He would never leave me to be Isaul's play thing, would he?

Quickly, I went through the motions of making myself presentable to be on Isaul's arm.

Before I even turned around Isaul grabbed my arm, his touch bruising as he dragged me out of the room and down the hallway.

"What's going on, Isaul?" I said, trying to tug my arm away from him. "You're hurting me."

He scoffed. "You'll see, sweetheart. You'll see."

Fear crept through me as I realized he must have discovered my transgression. He was going to punish me for shocking the nanobots for an hour. I should have known he would watch the video and find out. What was he going to do to me? Leave me in a dark room for days? Let his guards have a go at me?

But the strangest thing was, he would normally punish me after a deal was done. And Lyova was nowhere to be seen.

Where was he?

Fear crept through me, wondering if Isaul

blamed him for my little act of rebellion. "Isaul, please," I said, tripping over my feet as he hauled me onto a platform. The straps curled around me, holding me in place.

Isaul faced me, his hand cupping my cheek. "What do you think happened, my sweets?"

I shook my head, not wanting to give him any more information than he had to use over me. "I don't know," I whispered, feeling my eyes prickle with unshed tears. "Just," I licked my chapped lips, "where is Ly? What happened to him? Did I do something?"

Isaul tossed back his head, his laughter echoing against the metal plates of the buildings around us. The platform landed, sealing in place and the straps curled back into their sockets. He turned without answering, walking around the building and through a door. I cringed as the sirens blared, so loud I could barely hear myself think. The hallway was lit in crimson red. I gasped, stepping over blood staining the floor.

"Isaul, please," I begged. "Just tell me what happened."

I followed him inside a dark room. His guards filed inside and hovered near the walls. I couldn't see anything. I shrieked when the door slammed close behind me. Was this my punishment for buying the tonic? Darkness and alone with his guards?

"Lights," called Isaul, and the lights turned on.

I blinked for a moment, trying to adjust my eyes, shielding them for a moment. Images blurred together until finally I could make out the two men sitting in front of me. Their arms were tied behind them. Their legs chained to the floor. Both were bruised. One was bleeding from his nose.

He didn't look up at me. His head lolled from side to side, but I knew that mane. I knew that body.

I gasped, forgetting myself and lunging forward. "Lyova," I cried out, trying to go to him.

Isaul grabbed my arm and violently tugged me back. I whirled around shoving him away. "What the hell did you do to him?" I shouted.

Isaul smacked me. "You forget yourself, girl."

I held my cheek, feeling the sting rattle me. Straightening myself, I met Isaul's livid gaze and spat on the ground between us. "Let them go," I demanded. "They don't deserve any of this."

Isaul chuckled, moving to circle around Dorn and Lyova. "Oh really? Do you know what these idiots did?"

I didn't answer as Isaul nodded toward a guard standing near him. He stepped forward, his hands fisting at his side before he raised one and punched Lyova in the face. Lyova grunted, spitting blood on the ground. I covered my mouth, swallowing my sobs as my tears fell.

"Well?" Isaul shouted, whirling around to face me.

I took a deep, shuddering breath. "No," I whimpered, cringing out how broken I sounded. I took another deep breath and said in a stronger voice, "I have no clue what they did, Isaul."

Isaul laughed bitterly. "Did you hear that boys?" He strode over to Dorn. "She doesn't have any fucking clue what you did!" he shouted in Dorn's ear. He glanced back at me. "Should I tell her?"

The guards surrounding us nodded in unison.

"They destroyed my property. You know how much that cost me?" He shouted at Dorn and Lyova, grabbing and tugging harshly at their ears. "Millions! Millions you fucking assholes."

Dorn chuckled and Isaul nodded to the guard, who stalked over to him.

"Is that funny?" Isaul asked, his eyes bloodshot and manic. "You think fucking with me is funny?"

Dorn snorted, glancing at Isaul once again before breaking into laughter. "Quite," he gasped.

Isaul nodded to the guard, who kicked Dorn in the gut over and over again until Isaul shouted, "Enough."

Dorn fell over, gasping and clutching at his ribs.

"What the fuck do you think you were doing, huh?" Isaul asked as he continued to circle Lyova. "Were you paid by someone?"

Neither of them answered.

"Were you coerced by this fucking bitch?" Isaul pointed toward me, grabbing Lyova by his chin and lifting his gaze up toward me.

Lyova stared back at me. Bruises marred his eyes and his cheek. Dried blood caked his face. His hair was disheveled. My heart swelled and I wanted to run to him and take him away from all this.

"Did you find her cunt so delectable that you thought you could save her?"

Isaul stalked toward me, jabbing his finger into my face. "Did you tell them where the video comms were?"

It was my turn to rage. "How would I know where your little control room is Isaul? And besides," I leaned forward, not breaking eye contact and watching his eyes widen, "wouldn't you already know that? You watch every single little thing I do. Wouldn't you be able to plan for that?"

Isaul's teeth gritted and his fists shook at his sides before finally he released an angry yell. I stepped back, worried he would hit me again, or worse, but instead his yelling turned into obscene, crazy laughter. He slinked toward some pipes piled in a corner, grabbing one and dragging it across the floor toward Lyova.

"Isaul!" I shouted, already reading his mind and knowing what he had planned. "Stop! You're crazy! You don't know who they are. The Rodinian delegation is here for the Pax tournament. What would they say to torturing one of their citizens? Noble ones at that?" I lunged for him, but one of the guards grabbed my arms, pinning them behind me. I struggled against him, but he was too strong.

"That's the only thing keeping this one alive!" Isaul pounded the pipe against Lyova's shoulder. The crunch made me wince. "You think you can take my property from me!"

"Stop!" I shouted again as Isaul raised the pipe.

"From me!" Isaul shrieked, smacking Lyova in the back.

Isaul panted, the pipe lay on the floor. He handed it over to one of his guards. "Continue, please," he said as he straightened his cloak.

"No!" I shrieked, stomping on the guard's foot, but he only grunted. His hold on my arms didn't budge. "Stop, Isaul, this is madness. There's no reason to do this."

Isaul laughed. "No reason?" he said mockingly as the guard smacked the pipe against Lyova's back. "I have over a million reasons."

"But why, there would be no cause."

"Wouldn't there? What about the fact that this one might have gotten into his head to keep you for himself? Or maybe he and his little friend here are in fact Rodinian spies, sent to undermine the Pax. After all, there are plenty of them who serve in the Legion as soldiers. What they call Reapers." Isaul's face twisted in a cruel smirk. "For all you know, this one used you to get to me and all the information I had on all the senators here. Did you ever think of that?"

He signaled for the guard to hit Lyova some more.

"Don't!"

"Don't," Isaul mocked me.

"Stop, please. I will do anything."

Isaul held out his arm and the guard stopped midair. "Anything?" Asked Isaul with a twinkle in his eye.

I nodded. "Anything."

Lyova lifted his bloodied and bruised head. "Melisande, don't." He struggled against his restraints.

"Shut," Isaul said, kicking Lyova in the stomach, "up," he said with another kick. Isaul strode toward me, licking his lips. "Get on your hands on knees."

I picked up my skirts and lowered myself to the ground.

"Melisande, please," Lyova begged.

"Crawl to me and kiss my feet."

I crawled to him and gulped, staring down at his disgusting black shoes covered in dirt and grime. I closed my eyes and leaned forward, pressing my lips to each.

I looked up at Isaul in my bent over form, hoping what he saw appeased him. "Please let him go."

"Strip for me."

"Melisande, don't," I heard Lyova say. I didn't

want him to see me like this. I didn't want any of this for him.

I just wanted to have one moment.

I pushed at my dress, hearing the clang of Lyova's restraints echo in the air as he fought against them. Just how far would Isaul push this, I wondered briefly as I pulled my dress down and threw it to the side, kneeling before him in the cold, dank basement and waiting for whatever terrible thing he had in store for me.

Isaul crouched down, taking my chin in his. "Ah," he said, rubbing his thumb against my lower lip. "My poor little Melisande. How I hate to see you like this."

I shivered, sniffing. My lips trembled as I held back tears. I wouldn't let him see me cry.

"Remember that all that you have and all that you are is because of me and what I've given you," Isaul said, quickly standing. He nodded to one of his guards, who took off his jacket, throwing it on my naked shoulders.

Isaul turned around and circled Lyova, tapping his chin thoughtfully. "Unfortunately, I can't kill the great Lyova Artox without answering many, many questions. Plus, you do have quite a debt to pay off," Isaul snapped his fingers and another guard brought forth a large needle. Lyova fought against his restraints.

I sat there, not knowing what to do as two guards held Lyova down, injecting him with whatever concoction they brewed. "Ah, don't worry, Lyova," said Isaul, smacking his cheek lightly. "This won't kill you. You have to be alive and well, at least for your final fight in the morning."

Lyova slumped forward. The guards unchained him and as they moved toward him Lyova tried to attack but missed. Completely.

"What did you do to me?" He groaned.

"Nothing," Isaul shrugged. "Just gave you a little inhibitor. You have to earn back all my losses." Isaul smiled, crossing his arms. "With everyone else betting for you, oh undefeated Lyova Artox, I will make a killing when my bet against you earns me back a two thousand percent return."

Lyova groaned, trying to stand, but stumbling to the ground.

"No," I whispered, crawling toward Lyova.

I was so close. I just wanted to touch him, let him know I was here for him, do something for him.

"Ly," I called, my fingers so close to his cheek.

Isaul snatched my hand and pulled me up, toward him. "You are never to see him again."

"Let me go."

Isaul dragged me away from Lyova. I struggled against his hold, but he dragged me out of the room. "You are mine, and you need to earn your keep," Isaul shouted, slamming the door shut.

"Ly!" I shouted, but already the straps were wrapping around me and we were being pulled back toward the arena.

Isaul smirked, grabbing my chin. "You thought you could get away from me."

I jerked out of his hold. I didn't say anything as I watched the basement disappear from view, but I memorized the route, knowing I needed to get back to Ly. I needed to find a way to save him.

I needed a way to save myself.

I STARED OUT THE WINDOW, WATCHING THE sun rise over the city. I took a deep breath, trying to calm my nerves. I went over the plan, talking myself through everything. I just needed to get past the guards stationed at my door. Or rather, at Lyova's door.

I sniffed. He just wasn't here.

But I needed to see him. I needed to speak with him, come up with some sort of plan to get us out of this mess.

I pulled at the cord tied around my waist, making sure it was tight before pulling on it again. I tied the knot several times around the bed post, so it shouldn't untie. However, this was my first time sneaking out.

I smirked, thinking of Isaul. He always thought of himself as a genius mastermind, however, he didn't think everything through. And searching through Dorn and Lyova's things was a brilliant idea.

After Isaul dragged me away from Lyova he hauled me back up here, locking me inside and placing two guards at my door, just in case. But I wasn't in the mood to be Isaul's favored kept pet. In retrospect, I was a little shocked at all the weaponry, cloaking tech, and spy gear Dorn and Lyova had brought, but thankful that I could use it to escape my hellhole and get Ly out of this mess.

I opened the window, pushing it open all the way and took a deep breath as I looked down. We were on the eightieth floor. No big deal. I just needed to get to the floor below me. That was it. Just one silly floor.

Ignore the clouds and the idea of me splattering into the streets. I tugged on the rope again.

Oh, this was a bad idea.

I held onto the window, lifting a leg and resting it on the wall. I was wearing one of Dorn's boots, which seemed to suck on anything around once it was clicked on. I tested it out by walking around the walls of the room.

I lifted my other leg and placed it on the wall, trying to ignore the wind bursting around me, whipping my hair into my gaze. I held the rope with a white knuckled grip, saying a silent prayer that I would survive this while I slowly lowered myself.

"That's it," I muttered, "nice and slow."

Just hope the guards don't get any funny ideas and burst inside. That would really mess everything up.

I released the breath I had been holding when I was finally staring through a window. I grabbed the ledge, pulling my body onto it so I could finally sit. Not over yet, I told myself as I took a moment to let my legs stop shaking before knocking on the window rampantly.

There was no answer.

Oh, come on, it's freaking early. Someone must be in there. I knocked again. Loud. I pressed my hands against the glass and squinted, trying to find some sort of movement in the dark room.

A light turned on and an old Varon appeared, wrapping a robe around himself as he went to the door. I rolled my eyes and banged on the window again. "Not the door," I hissed, "the window."

The Varon looked around, scratching his bald

head while I banged on the glass again. His eyes widened when he found me sitting outside on the ledge, possibly scowling at him.

I made space as he opened the window, using the boots to angle myself before slipping inside. "Good gracious!" he exclaimed as I tumbled inside his room and untied myself.

"And a good day to you," I replied while stalking through the rooms. I saluted him before opening the door.

I walked quickly through the hallway, now brightly lit since the competitors and fans were now preparing for the final day of the tournament. I tried not to run; keeping my head down and pulling up the hood of Lyova's cloak, which seemed to swallow me whole. The sleeves were way too long, but it was nice feeling surrounded by his scent. It soothed me.

Not to mention it was a great way to hide myself. Sure, Isaul couldn't watch me anymore, but it didn't mean I was completely in the clear. He had spies and guards everywhere.

Even now he probably knew I escaped the room.

I needed to be quick.

I found the platform and got in line behind

several other Varons. I tapped my foot as I waited, glancing around me and wondering if Isaul's guards would just grab me out of nowhere. When it was my turn, I typed in the coordinates for the ground floor, waiting as the straps wrapped around me and surged below. I wanted to close my eyes, but I felt antsy, worry permeating through me that Isaul was having me followed, or that they were already waiting for me in the streets

The platform landed and I pulled the straps away from me, no longer able to wait. I threw open the doors, running through the brightly lit hallways. The blood had already been cleaned. When I came to Lyova's room, the door was already wide open. Broken chains hung from the doorknob.

"Lyova!" I shouted, terror seizing me that something awful happened, but I found him where I left him. Sitting in the center of the room with a collar around his neck.

But he was all alone.

Dorn was gone. His chains laid in a heap where he had been sitting.

"What happened?" I asked, kneeling in front of Lyova.

His head swayed from side to side and he groaned. I pushed his hair away from his eyes, cupping his face gently as I tried to get him to focus on me. "Ly," I whispered. "Are you okay?"

"Nope," he groaned, jerking away from me and lunging to the side, vomiting up green bile. "I feel absolutely terrible."

I rubbed his back when he gagged again.

"It's like something's in my head," he groaned, swaying and grimacing.

I pressed my forehead into his, pulling on his mane lightly. "You need to fight it."

Lyova swayed, leaning to the side, barely able to keep himself upright. Sweat glistened his temples. "I can't," he groaned.

I grabbed him, shaking his shoulders. His eyes fluttered closed. "Ly," I snapped my fingers in front of his face, hoping it would jar him awake. "Ly, I need you to focus. You must focus."

Lyova's eyes blinked open. They were having trouble focusing on me. He grabbed my cloak, leaning forward and bringing it close, smelling it. "Is this... mine?"

"Ly—"

Lyova chuckled. "You found our gear," he nuzzled his head into my shoulder. "You can finally escape, Melisande." He pushed me away from him. His touch was light. Too light. As if he had lost all his strength. "You should go. My team can track you while you wear my Reaper suit. You can finally be free, Melisande."

Reaper suit? Did that mean Isaul was right? Lyova was a one of the Legion Reapers? A super soldier type? I shook my head, focusing on what was important. At the moment, it was getting Lyova to safety. "I won't leave you like this."

Lyova rubbed his temples, inhaling deeply. "You must. It's the only way."

"No, it's not!" I shouted. Lyova was already drifting away, his eyes closing as his head lolled back. "Ly," I pulled him to me, smacking his face lightly. "Ly."

"Melisande," came a voice over comms. It was attached to Lyova's utility belt.

I grabbed the comms, holding it close to my mouth while pulling Lyova to me. He rested his head on my shoulder and I pet his mane. My fingers lightly touched his face. He was way too hot. I didn't want to think about what that meant.

"Dorn?"

"I'm here."

"Why the hell didn't you get Lyova out of here?" I shouted. If I saw that male, I was going to give him a swift kick in the shin.

"Do you know how heavy that bastard is?"

I stumbled backwards as Lyova leaned into me.

He had a point.

"Besides, they have no intention of killing him just yet, so I knew I had time. I'm looking for an antidote for that serum. That would be the best thing for him now."

"Well, hurry." I felt Lyova's forehead. Way too hot. What if the serum killed him? "I'm worried." Isaul would make Lyova fight in the tournament like this. He would be easy prey. Though the fights weren't to the death, accidents happened.

I shook my head, not allowing myself to think about him in that arena. I needed to focus. "This fight could kill him," I said calmly. "He's completely incapable of defending himself right now."

"Don't worry. I'm on it. Until then, whether you believe it or not, he is your true fated mate. A bond has already formed between you both. You can be each other's source of strength. Be strong for him now. You can do it. Keep this comm with you and I will get back to you with more info."

I tucked the comms into my cloak. Gently, I moved away from Ly, allowing his head to rest on the metal floor. "Ly," I said as I patted him lightly.

Lyova's eyes blinked three times before he finally was able to notice me. He smiled pulling me close to him and nuzzling his nose into the crook of my neck. "Melisande," he breathed.

"I have to go," I whispered, pulling his hands from me. "But don't worry, I'll get you out of this."

Be strong for him now.

Lyova pulled me to him. "Yes, go, be free my mate." He clung to me for a brief moment before falling onto the ground. I tucked a few stray stands behind his ear, petting him lightly before pushing myself up.

I couldn't help him while he was like this. Dorn said that he needed a cure. Maybe there was another source.

I stalked out the door. Maybe the doctor from the slums could help me. If he knew how to nullify Isaul's surveillance bots, maybe he knew about the serum that Isaul concocted.

THE DARKNESS WAS SWALLOWING ME WHOLE. I heard droplets hitting the metal floor in the deafening silence and the door creaking in the distance. My body felt heavy, as if a boulder was resting on my shoulders, weighing me down while hands pulled and held my limbs still. I groaned, opening my eyes at the sound of footsteps approaching, my vision blurring with dark shapes and shadows.

My head swayed back and forth, the movement making bile rise in my throat. I clamped my mouth shut, wincing at the nausea bubbling in the pit of my stomach. Fear crawled through me, snaking around my neck like a noose and I wondered if this was my life now. Whatever Isaul gave me.... Will it last forever?

My head moved violently back and forth. I heard shouting, shrieking, but I couldn't make out the words as if the serum had cut me off completely from the world.

"Wake up!"

Pain slammed through me as something hard hit my face, making my head whip around. I smacked the ground below, grimacing at the pounding in my head. I groaned, trying to push myself up, but remaining pathetically on the ground. Get up, Ly. But it didn't matter. The serum kept me pinned to the ground.

My eyes fluttered open, my vision blurring once more as dark shadows surrounded me. One large shadow grabbed me painfully by my arms and hauled me up. My feet scrambled underneath me. I held onto my captor, shaking my head and blinking several times until the world around me balanced.

I released the guard at my side, looking around at the dreary dark room. I sighed in relief when I spotted Dorn's chains lying in a heap, knowing he must have escaped. Hopefully, he found Melisande and got her out. Hopefully, they were already with Cade.

Isaul stepped in front of me. His yellow, bloodshot eyes were wide. Wide and wild as if he had completely lost his catnip. He smirked up at me, one long finger lifting my chin up, then back and forth as if he was assessing his latest product. If I had my strength, I would have lunged for him, bit off that finger and spat it in his face. I would have strangled that puny little throat of his; clawed his eyes out so he never laid them on Melisande ever again.

But my strength was long gone. Possibly forever. And I hated the way my body moved so willingly for him. I hated the lack of control I had. He had effectively taken my freedom completely away from me.

"Ready to earn me my money, Artox?"

I spat in his general direction, missing by a long shot. The bastard's lips curled into a wide, crazed grin. He patted the side if my cheek, treating me like a little kit having just learned to hunt prey.

Except this time, I didn't think I could pounce or lengthen my claws. I snarled, but it only came out as a pathetic whimper.

"Come alone now." Isaul turned on his heel, snapping his fingers to his guards.

The guards grabbed me on either side and hauled me through the white hallways. I hissed at the blinding lights, turning my head away and trying to stop the heat rushing through my body. What the fuck did he give me? I had never heard of a serum like this that had the power to take away one's strength or one's ability to remain conscious. Even now I felt my mind slipping into the darkness, heard it calling my name and seducing me back into its dark embrace.

I groaned as the polluted air met my face and the door slammed shut behind me. My legs stumbled to keep up. We weren't even moving quickly, yet my legs could barely support my weight. I opened my eyes, forcing them wide and awake. Stay awake, Ly. Don't fall asleep. Stay awake. I looked down at the platform below, watching as the electronic straps snaked out and around me, tightening their hold. Their bodies blurred, becoming scaled as red eyes gazed up at me.

I cried out, trying to move away from the serpents' hold. Their mouths opened, sharp fangs leering at me, about to strike. I pulled at the restraints, gasping in pain at the sudden movement. Isaul chuckled, his yellow gaze watching me, his grey face blurring into a faceless being.

"Where are you taking me?" I gasped, struggling as we flew higher toward the tournament.

The cheers from the crowds becoming louder and louder the higher the platform flew. I shook my head and willing the serpents away. Fight this, Ly. Don't give in to it. You need to fight it.

The fangs and red eyes disappeared and the straps returned to normal, but I was so exhausted. It took everything within me to see straight and keep the monsters inside at bay. Who knew how much longer I would remain conscious. I was slipping once more into that darkness. My head swayed from side to side.

"Why, we are taking you to your match of course." I groaned and tried to pull at the straps again. Wake up, Ly. "No need to thank me. You scratch my back, I scratch yours, isn't that right Lyova Artox?"

I bit back a gag when the platform jerked, the gears locking in place. The straps slid away from my body, leaving me shivering and swerving in place to keep my balance. I watched Isaul step down toward the crowd of people. Their curious gazes locked on me. I blinked as they all swirled before me.

Something shoved me forward and I stumbled down the steps. My feet were uncoordinated and rather than catching myself I went head first into the floor, landing sprawled out in front of the crowd of onlookers. I stumbled to stand, but my body remained glued to the floor.

Get up, Ly.

My body didn't budge. Not at all. The serum, whatever it was, shuddered through me and I felt it seducing me to back to an eternal sleep in the darkness. Just need to close my eyes for one moment, that voice inside my head teased. My eyes were already closing, my body was already becoming limp. I felt completely, and utterly lost within it.

"Oh, don't mind him," I heard Isaul. I didn't bother to look up. I nuzzled the floor, imagining I was elsewhere with Melisande.

I felt his guards haul me up, heard several onlookers whispering. My eyes fluttered open and I caught several female Varons whispering. They covered their mouths and eyed me with horror.

"He just had a bit too much to drink last night and fell." My feet dragged behind me as Isaul's guards took me down the ramp into the pit. "He'll be perfectly fine to fight!"

The doors slammed shut and I was thrown onto a bench. I leaned against the wall behind me, closing my eyes. Just for a moment. It's just for a moment. I'll regain my strength and then rip Isaul's arms off and shove him down that annoying little mouth of his.

"Lyova Artox!" Someone announced.

"Lyova, get up," someone patted my face.

I groaned, swatting them away. "Five more minutes," I muttered.

"Ugh, this drunken oaf."

I was grabbed and prodded into the bright lights, hissing when they burned my eyes. My vision was down to pinpoints of light in a sea of black. "Where am I?" I gasped, looking at the crowd rising like a wave around me.

It's the tournament, Ly. Get yourself together.

I inhaled deeply, hoping just breathing would send the serum out of my system. I waved half-heartedly as the fans cheered my name, smiling, but the movement was painful. I stumbled and landed sprawled on the ground. The crowd shushed and watched me push myself up from the ground. My muscles quivered with the exertion.

"Fuck," I muttered as I slowly pushed myself up.

I whirled around at the sound of a roar behind me. I watched for a minute too long as my opponent barreled toward me, claws bared. His face was contorted in an ugly snarl.

I stepped back, trying to break into a run or a pounce, but my body wouldn't budge. I barely had time to raise my arms in a block when his body came smashing into mine. I flew, feeling the wind underneath me before my back smacked the ground. I gasped for air; my breath tearing from my lungs.

Get up, Ly.

I tried to stand, but my opponent grabbed me by my mane and threw me into the ground. I heard a crunch at the sound of my nose breaking and whimpered. Blood ran down my nose. I cried out as pain racked my body; screaming when my opponent kicked me swiftly in my ribs. I rolled away, but I was too slow. He followed me across the ring, resting his foot against my back and slamming me back into the ground.

The robot hovered around me, counting down the numbers that would signal my defeat.

Ten.

Nine.

Eight.

My nails dug into the ground and I called out to the beast within me. Come on. I urged the red to enter my vision and strained my hands while I commanded myself to grow.

But my call went unanswered.

Seven.

Six.

Five.

I turned my head, ignoring the pain in my back as my opponent dug his foot into me. And that was when I saw her. Melisande.

I tiptoed through the hallways, peeking around corners to see if any of Isaul's goons were lurking nearby. I was being an idiot earlier, just waltzing in as if Isaul and his guards didn't have the place guarded. Although, in Lyova's state, I'm sure Isaul assumed he didn't need to be guarded. Lyova looked terrible. He could barely keep his eyes open. He barely knew I was even there. What was in that serum? I pushed down fear gnawing at the back of my head, whispering thoughts I really didn't want to think about right now.

What if it's permanent?

I gripped the comms in my pocket, knowing whatever it was, Dorn would discover an antidote.

He had to. I couldn't leave Ly like this. I didn't want him to suffer through the same fate I had.

That fate was reserved for Isaul, and Isaul alone.

I opened the door, peaking around the curved door, searching the streets for any sign of Isaul and his goons, but I saw no one. The streets were bare. Only trash and mildew lingered. It was completely silent except for the shouts and cheers of the tournament above. It wouldn't be long now. I need to hurry. Lyova could not go into the ring the way he was. His opponent would kill him. He wouldn't be able to defend himself.

Stop thinking about it and move!

I flicked my hood up and ran lightly into the streets. I moved on the balls of my feet, quiet like the air around me so as not to alert anyone to my presence. I kept my body low, my legs bent and trembling as I walked and I made a note to work out after all this. I peered around the large building, expecting to see an array of people moving in and out of the market, but it was so quiet. Why was it so quiet? That didn't make any sense. When I looked there was no one. Not a single soul. The stalls were completely empty and barren.

Where is everyone?

I continued walking through the dark stalls, looking over upturned tables in the hopes I'd find someone who could explain what happened. Tables were overturned, gadgets were smashed, chips were left it piles. The place looked like it had been ransacked. As if someone had been searching for something. As I went deeper into the market, I saw broken tables lying in piles in the small path through the market. Chips, visors, and ripped black cloaks were scattered everywhere. I stepped over the broken chairs and tables, biting my tongue when I saw blood smearing the ground.

What happened?

I stepped over the blood, tiptoeing through the mess, being careful not to touch anything that would ruin Dorn's boots. I ran toward the doctor's tent, finding it bent and crippled. I pushed away the cloak covering it, finding the doctor's broken body over the desk, his eyes staring back at me lifelessly.

I gasped, stepping back until I stumbled into something, or someone standing behind me. I jumped when hands gripped my arms, painfully, trembling despite myself as I felt breath on my neck, lips near my ear.

"Melisande," Isaul whispered, and I ground my

teeth to keep myself from screaming. He pulled my cloak down, his nose nuzzling my hair. He breathed deeply, caressing my face lightly. "What are you doing out? This place is dangerous." He chuckled as I tried to wrench myself free from him.

"Let me go," I rasped.

"We are going to be late, Melisande," said Isaul before tossing me toward his guards hovering behind him.

I struggled against them, stomping on one's foot and smiling when I heard his grunt. I jerked my shoulder from the other and elbowed him in the groin, but before I could get away, the other grabbed my hair and yanked me back. I screamed, kicking and shoving at anything that got in my way until my hands were pinioned behind me.

"Melisande, stop this." Isaul grabbed my face with one hand, squeezing my cheeks painfully as his face drew near, his disgusting breath swallowing my senses whole and making me gag. "Don't you want to see your love in action?"

At the mention of Lyova, thoughts pervaded me and an image of Lyova in the pit, lying broken and bloody with a crowd of onlookers; his lifeless gaze meeting my eyes. I sniffed, feeling tears welling inside me like a dam about to burst. And that's when I realized I was too late. Lyova was already taken. He was probably already in the arena now, getting kicked over and over again, his blood smearing the arena's floor.

What if he's already dead?

"Don't you want to see him, Melisande?"

I clenched my teeth, biting back a sob. Isaul nodded to his guards and I was carried onto the platform. I moved lifelessly, like a zombie being pulled and prodded through the crowd. The cheers were distant on my ears, as if my soul had already left my body. I closed my eyes when I saw the VIP box.

A front row view, Isaul? How kind of you.

Hushed whispers of the crowd met my ears. It had never been this quiet, not before when Lyova was fighting and I bit back another sob, not sure if I could look at his broken, lifeless body.

"Come now," said Isaul, patting my hand. "Don't you want to see your love, Melisande?"

I slowly opened my eyes, turning my scowl on Isaul. Tears dripped from my eyes, but I didn't bother wiping them away. Isaul rolled his eyes. "And here I thought I was doing you a favor," he muttered while his fingers gripped my chin and jerked me in Lyova's direction. "Take a look at what's become of your prized champion," he hissed in my ear.

Lyova cried out as his attacker kicked him in the ribs. He tried to roll over, to get up, but he was too slow. His opponent shoved his foot onto Ly's back and slammed him back down to the ground. I shoved away from Isaul and pushed through the crowd.

He wasn't dead.

Seeing him trembling there in the arena, I knew there was still a way to fix this. There was still a way to fight the serum coursing through Ly's veins. There had to be. His head lolled to the side, his breath coming out in pants. My breath hitched when his gaze met mine and soon, I found myself running through the crowd. I felt Isaul's hand on my wrist, but I shoved him off me. I ran to the edge of the VIP box, meeting Lyova's gaze.

"Get up!" I screamed at him, hitting the banister, but he remained on the ground, his face dirty with blood and grime. I shoved one leg over the bannister. "Get the fuck up!" I shoved the other over, but before I could run to him, I was pulled back into the box by one of Isaul's goons.

I held Lyova's gaze, and Dorn's words hit me. We had a bond. We were each other's source of strength. There was a way that I could be strong for Lyova, I could feel it in my gut. Inhaling deeply and sending whatever I possibly could through that little line that linked me to him.

You can do it, I whispered to him. Fight it. Fight the serum. I breathed in deeply, allowing myself to feel all the pent up anger over the years. The years of being Isaul's slave and allowing him to do whatever he pleased with me.

More. I wanted to give him more. So, I gave him all the love, all the heat, all the desperate longing that I had for him. I poured it all into the small connection that was between us.

And, I watched him stir.

Five.

Four.

Three.

My vision blurred red and my breath hitched as I felt a surge of something course through my body.

Unleash fucking hell, Ly.

Ly's fingers dug into the ground. I felt my energy swirl with his until suddenly, he caught his opponent's foot. The crowd gasped, watching Lyova shove his opponent, making him skitter through the arena.

Lyova slowly stood, his hands at his side, his tail whipping around him, his shoulders and arms tense with growing strength. His hands lengthened into long sharp claws and he crouched down low. A roar erupted through him, echoing throughout the crowd and he pounced, landing on top of his opponent.

The crowd cheered. Lyova's name rang out throughout the arena as he landed punch after punch into his opponent.

"Fuck this," I heard Isaul behind me and then he was tugging at my hair, yanking me back to him, his guards blocking my path.

"Ly!" I shouted, trying to pull away. "Ly!"

"You are mine!" Shouted Isaul as he dragged me away from the arena and through the emptied hallways. I fought against him, trying to rip myself from his hold. He grabbed my shoulder, slamming me against the wall. "You are my mate!" Shouted Isaul as he shook me. "Mine! Lyova will never have you."

I hissed in pain as my head banged into the wall behind me. Stars littered my vision.

Isaul's grip was painful as he grabbed my wrist, dragging me behind him. I clamped my eyes closed.

Ly, I called through the bond. *Ly, I'm being taken. Ly!*

I opened my eyes, tugging on my hand, smacking his hand, but Isaul refused to let go. I was being taken away and Ly wouldn't know until it was too late. Until I was far, far away, hidden deeper in the confines of space.

There was a beep on comms and I dug into my pocket, grabbing it and pressing it to my mouth. "Dorn!" I shrieked, ignoring Isaul as he whirled around and reached for me. "Help me!"

Isaul grabbed the device and threw it on the floor, stomping on it several times with his foot. He gasped, staring down at the broken device, before jerking his head up. His wide gaze found mine. His teeth grinding away and I knew there was no way I could go back with this male. I was not the same woman. I would never be that woman again. And I didn't care anymore what Isaul did to me.

I rolled my shoulders back, staring up at him as he scowled down at me, panting. His eyes were wide, bloodshot and crazed as paced back and forth. I didn't dare look away. I wouldn't allow him to scare me anymore. I could take care of myself, I realized that now. I didn't need him to keep the monsters of the streets away. He was the monster. He was the one who needed me.

Isaul raised his hand, the smack making my head whip back, but I still stared back at him, refusing to back down. He smacked me again, and I jutted my chin out. "Stop," he muttered, hitting me again. "Looking at me!"

I didn't look away.

His shoulders shook as he rolled his head back and forth, his hands fisting at his side. I didn't care. He was a weak, powerless male and I was stronger than him. He raised his hand again, but before he could hit me, I caught it in the air and shoved him away.

"How dare you!" Isaul roared.

"Melisande!"

I looked over Isaul's shoulder, smiling when I saw Dorn round the corner, holding a long gun. He kneeled, aiming it at Isaul, firing it and hitting him in the shoulder. Isaul gasped, staring down at the tip sticking out of him. I was sad to see it not go through the bastard's throat. He groaned, yanking out the arrow and throwing it on the ground, blood sputtering and staining the metal. Something clicked and beeped within Isaul, but I didn't have time to question it as Isaul snapped his fingers and his guards tackled Dorn to the ground.

Isaul grabbed my hand, tugging me away from the fight and I looked behind my shoulder, watching as one guard held Dorn while the other punched him in the face. I was shoved onto the platform, the straps tying me into place and I scowled at Isaul as we left the level, surging upwards and into the sky, the wind making my hair float all around me.

Ly, I tried again through the bond. *Ly, please come for me. Please find me.*

I whirled around, my foot digging into my opponent's neck, but I ignored his gasps and pleas as I scanned the VIP box, finding no sign of Melisande nor that bastard Isaul. I jerked my attention down on my assailant, no longer in the mood to wait around for the bastard to pat the ground or for the robot to call out zero. I shoved my foot deeper into his neck, his eyes bugging out while his hand patted the ground three times.

"Lyova Artox wins!" Shouted the robot and the crowd erupted into cheers. Fireworks burst through the air while holographic flowers rained down all around me.

I ran toward the VIP box, dodging the robot hovering around me, about to offer me congratulations. Usually there was an interview after these tournaments, but fuck that. I need to find her. I must find her. If I didn't—

"Lyova Artox!" Called the stupid robot. I ignored it as I jumped over the VIP box and pushed my way through the crowd.

"Lyova Artox!" The robot shouted, following me into the hallway, spilling the crowd inside with each minute that passed. I looked from side to side, inhaling deeply. Her scent was vague, but still there.

"Mr. Artox if you would-"

I whirled around and grabbed the metal hunk of junk by its scrawling little throat, dragging it close to my elongated teeth.

"What?" I growled, barely containing myself from ripping it to pieces.

"Nothing, nothing," said the robot, holding up its electrical hands while tugging itself away.

I released its throat, watching it slowly back away from me before skittering through the air back to the arena. I growled as I tried to find Melisande's scent, which was becoming polluted by the many aliens leaving the arena.

Ly, please come for me. Please find me.

I felt her tug on the bond and bolted into a run,

following that tug around the corner where I found Dorn fighting off two of Isaul's goons. Poorly. It looked like the assholes broke his nose. Blood was pouring down from it while he side-kicked one in the face. The other grabbed his arm, throwing him over his shoulder, but before he could turn around Dorn was already in a crouch, sweeping his opponent's feet from underneath him.

Dorn paused, standing between the two guards as they groaned and stumbled to stand. He scowled at me, hands on his hips. "Well I'm glad you're feeling better. So, are you just going to stand there, or are you going to help me?"

I lunged, grabbing the guard on Dorn's right and slamming his face into the wall. Dorn pounced on the other, slamming him into the ground and punching him in the face several times before his head lolled to the side.

I helped Dorn up, watching him wipe the blood from his nose, gasping for breath. "Finally," Dorn said, digging into his pockets for his comms. "They were surprisingly adept."

"Where is she?"

"He's taking her to the docking station." Dorn clicked comms. "Is everything set?"

I watched Dorn stand there, as if he had all the

time in the world. As if he didn't know Isaul was about to take my mate away and hide her deep within the galaxies. "What's going on?"

Dorn smiled in my direction. "Don't worry, Ly. We're on it."

"Affirmative," came Cade's reply on comms. "Everyone is in place."

Dorn shoved comms back into his pocket and rubbed the back of his head. He glanced at me, offering a small smile. "The things I do for you, Ly," he said, before breaking into a run down the hallway toward the platform.

"Dorn!" I shouted, coming up behind him. "What exactly is going on?"

"Come on, slowpoke," he called, laughing over his shoulder. "Let's go save your mate."

Dorn waited for me at the platform, typing in the coordinates while straps wrapped around us. The platform unhinged and we were flying up the tower. Flying higher and higher through the clouds and even higher after. The wind rushed behind me and even though we were flying fast and high, it still felt like an eternity passed until we were at the top, docking the helipad with Legion surrounding the area.

I looked around the familiar and unfamiliar

faces. How are they even here? I wondered, pushing through the crowd of Rodinian reapers until I spotted Cade and Isaul in a standoff at the center. He was holding Melisande close to him, like a shield as he shuffled toward the aircraft behind him.

"No!" I shouted, stalking toward them.

Melisande stomped on Isaul's foot, earning a hiss, but still he held her tightly in front of him. I didn't know what to do. He could easily throw her into the aircraft and leave. He could throw her from the tower. And all I could do was stand and watch, hoping the bastard would simply let her go.

"Give it up!" Cade shouted, stepping forward. "We have you surrounded Isaul Reene. Let her go."

Isaul chuckled. He nuzzled her hair, pushing its whipping strands behind her ear. His gaze caught mine and his smile widened. Parting his lips, his long tongue licked her cheek.

I would enjoy ripping that appendage from his body.

Isaul shoved Melisande in front of him, jerking her toward the edge of the tower. "Be very careful, Lyova Artox!" Isaul shouted over the bustling winds. "I would hate for her to take a tumble."

I stopped. Rooted in place. Unable to do

anything but watch as he pulled her toward the aircraft.

Cade sighed, turning around. He nodded to the other commanders. "Ready!"

Everyone lifted their blasters, the red beams aiming for Isaul's head. Isaul stopped, his eyes flickering up, down, back and forth; eyeing all the beams aimed for his head.

"Let the female go," Cade called over the wind, a devilish smile on his lips as he stepped forward. His hands rested casually behind him. "Or we'll blast your ugly little face off. Your call, Reene."

Isaul scowled. His nails dug into Melisande's arms. For a moment I didn't think he'd let her go. I calculated the distance to the tower's edge, already readying myself to lunge if he did decide to toss her. But something in Isaul must have changed, because instead he sighed, his hands slowly releasing her arms. I blinked. Not believing what was happening as Isaul raised his hands over his head.

Melisande watched Isaul while taking a step from him. Then another. And another. Until finally she was running to me and I was running to her, flinging my arms open to pull her against me. I swung her around several times, pulling her closer and enjoying her being near me once more.

"Ly!" She cried, nuzzling her face against my shoulder, gripping me tightly. "I didn't think I would see you again," she whispered against my flesh, her tears wetting my neck.

I stroked her hair, her face, lifting her chin up so I could get a view of her tearstained face. "I would never allow him to take you, Melisande. Never. You are mine." I pulled her back to me, never wanting to let her go. Ever.

I turned my gaze from the top of her head to watch Cade. He was approaching Isaul with the electric bands to bring him in. Isaul smiled at me, his hands still raised high. He cocked his head to the side when Cade reached for him, but before the bands met his flesh, he kicked Cade in the shin and ran. The bastard ran to the edge of the tower and jumped, landing on an aircraft speeding away.

"Fuck!" Shouted Cade, running after Isaul, but stopping at the towers edge. The aircraft was too fast. It would take too long and it was worthless to follow him.

Dorn chuckled, taking a GPS tracking system out of his utility belt. "Don't worry," he waved. "I injected him with a modified version of his bots earlier." He clicked several buttons and smirked. "He's already transmitting to our comms. We'll be able to find him easily."

As if on cue, fireworks burst high above us, flags rising in the clouds below and coming into view, waving all around. The chant of *Lyova Artox* surged from below.

"I take it you won after all?" Melisande smiled up at me, a twinkle in her eye.

"Of course, I did." I nuzzled her nose.

"Then you should go and collect your prize," she whispered against me.

I shook my head, stroking her face. I couldn't stop touching her. I didn't want to. "I already have my prize," I whispered before claiming her lips.

I SAT IN THE MEDICAL BAY, WATCHING A human girl named Callie look over my injuries while Talus cut my mating cuffs with a small torch. Lyova stood at my side, my ever present knight in shining armor. He stroked my hair absentmindedly, as if I was a cat, he was using to relieve his stress. We arrived on the Aurum yesterday, and shortly after meeting everyone, Lyova had whisked me away to the medical bay. I guess I couldn't blame him. I was a complete mess. My face was red and bruised, I hadn't slept since I was woken by Isaul, and there were bruises up and down my arms.

Thankfully, all gone now due to several hours

lounging in the vat, having my aches and pains mended by the blue gel.

The doors slid open and I flinched, my hands gripping the armrests as I waited for Isaul to enter with his guards and take me away. Instead, Solana entered, smiling at me while striding over. "Hi!" She called, her smile faltering and I realized I was digging my nails into the armrests.

I forced myself to let go and smile back. He won't get you here. Everything is fine.

Lyova kissed the top of my head. "Are you all right?"

"Perfectly fine."

I was thankful when he didn't press me. With one final stroke of the torch the last of my mating cuffs fell from my wrists with a clink on the floor.

"Well, that's it," said Talus while lifting up his visor. "You're a free lady." He winked at me before leaning over Callie and looking at my diagnostics. "How is she, Cal? Good to go?"

Callie smiled, pocketing her reader. "Yep." She chuckled when Talus wrapped his arms around her, resting his chin on her shoulder.

"I'll give you the tour once you are well rested," said Solana, giving me a wink over her shoulder as she strode over to Dorn, currently sitting in a vat similar to mine and touching his newly healed nose.

My face heated and my gaze moved to Lyova, who smiled sheepishly down at me. Yeah... well rested. So that's what the kids are calling it these days.

"Well," began Callie, shrugging Talus off her. "The bruises healed well, but-" she raised one finger, "I think you should have a talk with someone when you are ready. Some scars aren't seen." She gave me a knowing look and I nodded. "But only when you're ready. I'm here," she smiled and patted my hand. "Let me know if you need anything."

The door slid open again and I flinched, this time forcing myself to keep my hands in my lap. He isn't going to come for you, I told myself as Cade entered through the door.

"Hey, how are you?" He asked, sidling up next to Solana and kissing her cheek.

"I'm fine," I said, not knowing what else I could possibly say.

"I like how no one has cared to ask about me," said Dorn while typing something into his tablet. He didn't bother looking up as he scowled at the device.

"Did you find anything on that serum, Dorn?" Asked Cade, strolling over to him.

Solana rolled her eyes. "Can't you let the poor man rest for a moment?" She followed Cade over to Dorn. "And how are you Dorn? Is your nose ok? You sure do get a lot of head injuries."

Dorn smiled in Solana's direction. "Perfectly fine. Thanks for asking, Solana." He turned his direction to Cade. "And, this really can't wait." He sighed, rubbing his temples. "It's highly possibly Isaul acquired the serum from the Kridrins." His gaze narrowed. "And it is also highly likely that Isaul isn't their only client."

"Fuck," muttered Talus while smacking the wall.

Dorn nodded. "They may be attempting to neutralize the Legion collective through the alphas. After all, most of the warriors that serve are alphas. There is evidence that the Kridrins and the Sovereign Worlds are colluding." He cleared his throat. "All this is suspect, though. But the information is compelling enough to take to Commander Batair."

Cade nodded. "Agreed. Anything else?"

Lyova took my hand, helping me down from the vat and into his arms. I yawned, leaning my head against his chest, enjoying the mere warmth of him by my side.

"I'm going to take Melisande to our quarters," called Lyova, already moving us to the door.

Cade smiled. "Of course, Ly. We'll fill you in with the details later."

I allowed Lyova to lead us back, following him down the long white hallway. I paused in front of a shimmering window, taking in the stars and darkness that seemed to swallow us whole. I had spent these last few years on the Sovereign Worlds, drifting back and forth between the city planets, polluted with space trash and satellites. I had never seen such a space so vast and open. I felt tears prickling my eyes at the thought.

I was finally free.

"Melisande," Lyova breathed.

I glanced over my shoulder, smiling while wrapping my arms around him. We continued down the curved hallway until doors parted for us and I was standing in a completely different room. A room that seemed so completely and totally Ly.

There was a cot next to the shimmering window and a table cluttered with electric swords, throwing knives, torn apart guns, and holographs of Rodinians I could only assume were his family back home. Clothes sat in a heap around the room, and I watched with a chuckle as Lyova scattered around the room, quickly picking them up and throwing them into the small closet space he had.

"Sorry," he muttered, rubbing his head. "I'm not the most--"

I cupped his face, going on my tiptoes and brushing my lips against his. "It's fine," I whispered.

He moaned against my lips, pressing them harshly against me. His tongue stroked my bottom lip while I coaxed him toward the bed. He stumbled, falling backwards and I moved my legs to straddle him. I sat above him, looking down at him for a moment and knowing there was no rush. I didn't have just an hour with my mate. I didn't have to worry about Isaul watching me or his guards entering this room.

I could take my time with him.

My hands pulled at his shirt, pressing under the fabric to feel his muscles. He pulled his shirt over his head, throwing it across the room. His lips sought mine, his hands tugging me down so he could capture me, but I pushed him down with a firm hand, pinning him to the bed. I knew he was stronger than me; knew he could easily me roll me over and take what he wanted. Instead, he lay there, watching me with curious eyes and a slightly parted mouth.

I wanted him begging for it.

I continued stroking his abs, my fingers stroking a line up and down his chest, exploring the contours of his body. His breath hitched when I dipped down, my tongue teasing his nipple before I swallowed it whole and gave him a teasing bite. His hands pulled at my shirt and I obliged, shrugging out of the garment while pressing tender kisses into his chest.

"You are so beautiful," Ly whispered, his hand stroking my hair, and brushing it away from my face, behind my ear. I looked up, meeting his golden gaze, my face heated with want and need. "Absolutely beautiful."

"I know about the bond between mates," I said tentatively. "What do I need to do to make it happen?"

"You don't have to worry about that now," he said. Even as he said it, though, there was a thrumming between us that I couldn't quite describe. It was like a buzzing as if he couldn't contain his excitement.

Good. That meant that he wanted to be with

me as much as I wanted to be with him. "I'm not worried. I just know I want to you more than anything I wanted in my entire life. And the thought of being apart horrifies me."

He pulled me against him. "No power in this universe can keep me away from you." His vow shook me down to my very soul. Every cell in my body claimed that promise of his.

I straddled his hips. "Good, now tell me how we do this."

"Bonding starts with you. You start it by taking me into your tight little pussy," he emphasized by flicking his thumb over my clit. I swallowed a groan, feeling myself grow hot and slick under his attention. "And when you feel the pull of our bond, you bite me. And then I bite you."

I gasped as warm waves of pleasure coursed over my body. "Bite? Will it hurt?"

"You will be so full of me that you won't even notice."

"Is that so?" I teased.

He chuckled. "You're already open and wet for me, kitten, it's too late to deny that."

I fell into his kiss, his tongue stroking mine. I lined my body up with his and took his tip into my entrance. He gripped my thigh but did nothing else, though every muscle in his body tensed beneath me. The power that I had over him was heady and turned me on more than anything else did.

I let gravity take over as I took his massive length inside my body. When he was finally seated inside me completely, I was incoherent with pleasure. Every single ridge pulsed against my inner walls, stretching me, hitting every pleasure point just right. I barely had to move, and I was feeling the grip of a massive orgasm starting deep inside of me.

That was it, that pull that he talked about. My teeth ached to sink into flesh. My nails were already deep in his shoulder. I hoped I wasn't hurting him.

I gazed down at him through my lashes, and his golden eyes were molten pools of desire. It was taking all of his discipline to restrain himself from moving against me.

Damn, that was humbling, seeing such a large male wait for me to make my choice.

I followed the pull of the bond as it pushed me forward, coaxed me to mark him. He was mine. I sank my teeth into his neck, pressing down until I tasted his blood.

A rush of pleasure surged through me, and I screamed against him, rubbing clit against the ridges at the base of his cock.

Lyova's hand dug into my hair and held me in place as he bit the delicate skin of my neck. Another wave of pleasure coursed through me. Hot slick bathed his cock as he thrust up inside of me. I tightened around him, and he moved flipped us over so that he was on top, hammering against me like a mighty piston.

Liquid heat exploded within me as I completely lost control. I clawed his arms, my nails sinking into his shoulders as I gasped.

"Lyova," I shouted as another wave of pleasure hit me and I was thrusting myself against him, unable to stop my body. Not wanting to stop. "Lyova," I screamed as pleasure so great smacked into me and gripped my body. I was shaking, but I couldn't stop. He was thrusting so hard and so deep inside me, cradling me to him, kissing my face over and over again. My name on his breath.

I didn't know how long we lasted. We couldn't stop touching each other, couldn't part our bodies from one another.

A lifetime wouldn't be enough with him.

I FLIPPED THROUGH THE CHANNELS ON THE screen while I waited for Melisande to finish with her shower. The prowler hummed around us, filled with newly acquired clothes Solana and Callie had put together for Melisande.

I was excited for this next mission with her. Destination: Honeymoon.

Excited for this life we now shared together, filled with exploring the vast space and each other's bodies. It was nice to see Melisande finally let go and be herself. The first few days were a bit hard. Well, after we finally left our room. The bedroom stuff wasn't difficult at all, but she was quiet. Reserved. Taking everything in with a quiet shock. I was extremely grateful Solana and Callie took her under their wing with Solana giving her a tour of the Aurum and Callie showing her the tech room. It was good to see her laugh so easily.

But there were times she would stare off into space. Looking expectantly at the door, as if someone would come to take her away. And I knew in those moments she was waiting for Isaul to return for her. I didn't know what to say or do. She seemed so quiet, so resolute. I wanted to kiss it all away. Tell her I would never allow him to take her away from me. Solana told me it would take time. Callie told me it was highly possibly Melisande's fear would never go away. But time would help.

Time always helped.

It broke me to awaken in the middle of the night, hearing her crying as some dream from long ago haunted her. And I would simply pull her into my arms and kiss her tears away. It was lessening with the passing weeks.

I glanced over my shoulder, smiling as her voice carried over the water. She was singing some Terran song I had never heard before. Terrible singing voice, but it was good to know she was happy.

And I would help her through the good times and the bad.

I turned back to the screen, flipping through the channels once more, hoping to find something interesting. It seemed like there were only ads. Ads for the latest and greatest outposts. Bounty hunter ads. I stopped when I saw my picture on the screen.

Oh no!

"And for the next news we have the Sovereign Worlds Gladiator Tournament meant to establish peace between the Varons and the Rodinians," said the male reporter with green skin, dressed in a putrid yellow suit.

The female sitting next to him wore the same putrid yellow color but had purple skin. "I wonder how that turned out," she said enthusiastically with an eerily cheerful smile.

The view changed to one of me, being dragged into the arena by several other competitors. "No," I moaned, tugging my mane and scowling at the screen.

"What is it honey?" I heard Melisande behind me.

I glanced over my shoulder, for a moment stunned by Melisande's beauty. She was drying her long red hair with a towel, dressed in simple shorts and t-shirt. I have the most beautiful female in the galaxy.

"Oooh! It's the tournament," she said with a wide smile, tossing her towel in the corner and striding toward me. She wrapped her arms around my shoulders, setting her chin in the crook of my neck. Her scent washed over me. I didn't think I could ever get used to its calming effect. It was like a magical moonlit evening on a lake.

"Oh, I guess Lyova Artox had a few too many drinks the night before," came the announcer's voice, ruining that magical feeling and drawing my scowl back to the screen.

"I didn't have too much to drink!" I shouted. "I was poisoned!"

Melisande patted my shoulder. "I know."

"But they don't know that!" I groaned again, watching my sorry ass sway back and forth in the middle of the crowd filled arena. I watched myself raise my hand, trying to smile. "Star's blazes, I look half dead. Clearly, I should not have been fighting."

I rubbed my face. I didn't know if I could watch any more of this. It was enough to live through it, but to have it on intergalactic television for everyone to see. I gasped, watching my opponent throw me across the arena as if I weighed nothing more than a tablet.

"Oooh," said the announcer. "That looked like it hurt."

I crossed my arms. "It did!"

Melisande chuckled behind me. She kissed the top of my head before sidling up next to me and sitting herself in my lap. "I'm so happy it didn't have any lasting effects," she whispered in my ear, nipping my lobe and kissing a path to my jaw. She pulled away, waggling her eyebrows at me with a coy smile.

I growled, pulling her closer to me. "You and me both, kitten."

I drew her lips to mine, sucking on the bottom and with a small gasp my tongue entered to stroke hers. She tasted amazing. Her tongue prodded mine, lighting a fire within me. Her scent swallowed me whole and I wanted to bury myself into her. My hand slid up her thigh, playing with her waistband. Let this idiots think what they want. I have my mate and that's all that mattered

"In other news, Isaul Reene has been cornered at..."

Melisande stopped. I opened my eyes, watching her withdraw at the name. Her face turned away from me and she stared at the screen with wide, fearful eyes. She sat up in my lap, her hands digging painfully into my neck.

"Yes, after a long shoot out which left many of his soldiers dead, Isaul Reene was brought into custody and will be facing trial for illegal use of surveillance bots, blackmail, tampering—"

I turned off the screen. Melisande stared into the blackness, her mouth slightly agape. I caressed her face, waiting for her to turn to me, but she sat still, her skin paling. I waited. I didn't want to force her into talking about it. It was her choice. I would always be there for her to listen. I stroked her hair, massaged her shoulders until I felt the tightness lessen and she was leaning against me. Her hands slid down my chest, her face burrowing into my shoulder. Her arms wrapped around me. She didn't sob. She didn't say anything. All she did was hold onto me.

"I want to see him," she said finally.

Out of the question. I didn't want to say the words aloud, knowing they were wrong. Callie suggested I listen to Melisande when it came to Isaul's abuse. My mate came first. Always. "Do you think that's a good idea?" I asked, rather than shouting the *hell, no* that I would have preferred.

Melisande was silent for a while, her body still against me as if she had fallen asleep. I was about to say something but stopped when I felt her slow nod. "I think it will be good for me." She pulled away and wiped her eyes. "I can finally get some closure, Ly."

I didn't know. I didn't want her ever seeing the bastard again. I didn't want her to cry and have that look on her face anymore, but would this really help?

"Ly?" She gazed at me with pleading eyes.

I sighed. She nuzzled my nose and I knew she had already won. "Fine. But I go with you."

I WALKED THROUGH THE BLUE HALLWAYS OF the prison outpost, Corux, with Lyova at my side.

The lights flickered with our movement. The prisoners watched with curious glances behind their force field cells. There was barely enough room in each cell for each prisoner to move. They were dark with one toilet in the corner.

No privacy here.

Funny how this reminded me of my own accommodations.

"You'll only get a few minutes to speak with him," said the guard as he led us down the long hallway.

I flicked my hair behind me. "A few minutes will be more than enough, thank you." It wasn't like we were old best friends wanting to catch up for a cup of coffee.

I just wanted to see him. I wanted to know he was here and know he was suffering the same fate he had forced on me. Especially now that he was locked in a cell with no privacy. Constantly watched. Constantly surveyed. No conversation a secret. His body no longer his.

It was no secret on the Aurum how Isaul had used me. And it was something I still wasn't ready to talk about. I glanced at Lyova and felt my heart swell at the intense emotion I felt through our bond. I might not be ready to talk about my past, but with us, we didn't need words.

"Don't get too close to the force field," continued the guard, glancing over his shoulder. "It's just a security measure. He can't get out."

I nodded. Looking down, I found Lyova's fingers lacing with mine. The warmth and his scent calming whatever darkness was seeping out of me. "You're doing great," he said, pushing a loose strand of my hair behind my ear. "I'm here if you need anything."

We turned a corner and I stopped, already seeing Isaul's gray form in his dirty and torn cloak. I shivered at his yellow gaze staring back at me, the curl in his lips as I drew closer. One eye was black and his nose was broken. There were cuts along his face and I suspected there were more all over his body. His neighbors sat in their beds, scowling at us, but made no move to hide their blatant eaves-dropping.

"Ah, Melisande," said Isaul, strolling toward the force field between us as if he was having a lovely day at the zoo. His cloak was down, the hood must have been cut off and I could see the bald patches in his thin white hair. "What a pleasure to see you again."

I didn't say anything. I looked him up and down, taking in this dirty and broken male. There was mildew on the hem of his cloak. His fingers were caked in grime. His face seemed gaunter than before. He paced back and forth in front of the shimmering shield while I eyed him silently.

"Has my pet come to torment me?" He laughed, his eyes wide and bloodshot. I kept myself rooted, fighting through the horror I felt, the worry he was going to take me away.

He couldn't get out. The guard said that. He would be stuck in here forever.

"I just wanted to know," I finally said, crossing my arms in front of me.

Isaul turned around, raising his hands above his head. "Like what you see?"

I nodded. "I most definitely do." He opened his mouth, but I was quick. "Now you know how it feels to be caged. Oh, and you get to be the one wondering what will happen to you in the middle of the night. If you get surprise visitors. If you, I don't know, get dragged from here to meet an even worse fate."

Isaul ran toward the force field, reaching out as if he would smack or grab me. I didn't flinch. I didn't move. I watched as he was shocked by the electrical fields. He shrieked and fell backwards. The beginning of a red welt was already forming on his singed hands. Isaul cradled his injury, scowling up at me while pushing himself up. "I gave you everything," he hissed.

"You gave me nothing." I tightened my grip on Lyova's hand. "Goodbye, Isaul."

With one last look, I turned around and walked down the hallway with Lyova at my side.

"You come back here; you bitch!" Isaul shouted behind me. I just kept walking. I didn't turn around. I forced myself to face forward. He didn't deserve any more attention that what I'd already given him. "You come back here and you fix this.

Because of you I lost everything. Everything! You hear me!"

I smiled as we turned the corner. "You did great," said Lyova, squeezing my hand gently.

I pulled him toward me, stroking his mane. I felt like I was on top of the world, like I could finally let go and start a new life. I stroked Lyova's face. "Thank you," I breathed, touching his forehead with mine and breathing him in.

A new life with my mate.

The end of *Prized*.

Check out *Freed,* the next book in The Legion: Savage Lands Sector.
(https://evangelinepriest.com/book/freed-the-legion-savage-lands-sector-3/)

While you wait for the next book, if you liked this book, please leave a review. I would appreciate any kind words, even a short sentence or two.

The feedback and support would mean the world to me as I continue to write this series.

About the Author

Eva Priest writes otherworldly romances with strong heroines and the dominant alpha males who claim them.

You can sign up for Eva Priest's newsletter HERE or enter this link into your favorite web browser: (https://evangelinepriest.com/newsletter).

She is excited to share excerpts, cover reveals, and exclusive content at least once a month.

Follow Eva Online

www.evangelinepriest.com

Amazon

Bookbub

Facebook

Instagram

Twitter

THE OUTPOST WAS OLD, DARK, AND DANK. IT was a floating derelict that reminded me of the skeletal remains of a felled creature. The force field that surrounded the once bustling city was still intact. The holographic clouds drifted past a sea of stars with only ghosts as their witness.

It was the perfect drop site for smugglers.

A series of beeps tapped against my wrist from my gauntlet. I was getting closer to the stash of goods that Silar Praxis had negotiated on the Legion's behalf. Funny how mere months ago, Legion command had tasked my squad for hunting that smuggler down, and now here I was protecting him.

Slipping through shadows, I found myself at

the mouth of a tunneled pathway. My head grazed the low ceilings as I approached my target. I curled my lip as the musty scent of dead air managed to seep through the multiple filters of my Reaper suit's rebreather. Water drips echoed from unseen pipes, and I ignored the urge to track down the leaks and fix them.

The tunnel spilled out into a nearly empty arena. We had decided that this would be the best place to make the transfer. Easy in, easy out. I checked my coordinates once more. My prowler blipped onscreen, indicating where I had parked it underneath the stadium seating opposite from where I stood. Another ping hit dead center from the middle of the arena.

The supply cargo for the Legion colony.

At least the supplier had lived up to their part of the bargain. Now to make sure that there wasn't any funny business. I activated my scans for any triggers or traps. When my retinal screen reported an all-clear, I let out a breath. I activated my comms to hail the two recruits I was training in the field. "Reaper Two to Away team. What's your status?"

"All quiet, Reaper Two," Markus's eager voice boomed over the comm. "Aside from your pings and activity, I see nothing moving on the surface."

I addressed the other recruit who was supposed to be on the lookout for possible ships. "Liam? What about you?"

"Can confirm. No other signs of life."

"Any sign of the Lucky Duck?" I asked.

"No sir."

A moment later, a high-pitched scree wailed over the comms. I muted the line before the sound deafened me. Before I could bellow out an order, the signal lights for the Lucky Duck turned on full. They were practically on top of me, slowing down as they approached the surface.

I took my comms off mute, and as expected, it was full of wild chatter from both Liam and Markus. At least I was used to calming down excitable warriors to focus on the mission priority. "Report."

"Shit, Reaper Two, we didn't realize they were that close."

"Nothing came over on the sensors? No readings?" My sensors hadn't alerted me either, otherwise I would have had a very different response for these recruits.

"Not even a blip, sir."

"Affirmative," Markus added. "Nothing on my scanners. I would have seen."

Markus's earlier enthusiasm had dimmed a little. The boy would have more than enough reasons to become hardened and jaded as a Reaper. I wouldn't let that happen while he was still under my command, though.

"I believe you, recruit. There was nothing on my sensors either. This is why we have teams. We watch each other's backs. Remember that. Come in tight. No reason to be on the look out when we might not even see what's coming. Let's keep an eye on those we can see."

I listened for their confirmation as they began maneuvers to come in closer to the surface. It was a good thing that more Reapers had been assigned to the Aurum. Soon, it will be a warship of note, and we might get an upgrade.

Speaking of upgrades, the Lucky Duck sure had one. I eyeballed the boxy craft as it touched down. It wasn't flashy or sleek, but then again, that was the point. Smuggling vessels were meant to blend, not stand out. Even so, it was more than it had been a few months back.

It had been patched up, overhauled, and apparently, they've added new cloaking tech. My hands itched to check out their engineering bay to see how they crept up to a Reaper team completely undetected.

The landing pods opened and two males stepped down from the loading bay.

"You're late," I said by way of greeting. I didn't need to raise my voice for it to carry around the arena.

"What are you, my date?" The gray-skinned male looked up at me. He had the carefree air of a child, what with his lanky build and ridiculous pouf of orange hair that seemed to defy gravity. But he was every bit a combat-hardened soldier. It was in his eyes, which narrowed at me with annoyance.

"I'm here, that's important. Now are you gonna bitch or are you ready to work?"

Silar was getting too comfortable if he thought he could speak that way to a Reaper. I answered with a low-level growl that reverberated through the air.

At least his head of security still valued his life, since the burly male sucked in air through his teeth. "Uh, let me get the pallet jacks activated," the male said, and scurried off to make himself useful.

I smiled extra wide to make sure he got a hint

of fang. We had the reputation of being ruthless killing machines, and I didn't want to disappoint.

After the Pax tournament, which took place on the Concord of Sovereign Worlds, we obtained intel about a conspiracy threatening the entire Legion collective. The more we could maintain a "don't mess with us" vibe, the more we could avoid needless bloodshed.

Apparently, there were those of the Sovereign Worlds who would rather push for an outright war rather than continue to pretend to be allies. Worse, those shadow groups were working with the yet unknown Kridrin.

Though we have seen directly the harm the Kridrin could do, no one knew anything about them. Not their origin, motives, or even their biology. They somehow appeared on our radar only a few months ago, and yet, they seemed to be behind every shady business around.

The worst offense being slave trading. More and more reports of trafficked females have been popping up, and it had spread our resources thin over this sector.

All of this had made it necessary for us to take precautions, because it had become apparent that there were more enemies in secret than we realized, and we needed to be careful, including being careful with whom we did business.

When his crewman was out of sight, Silar Praxis rolled his eyes. "You know how hard it is to convince my crew to work with you guys, and now here you go acting like that, I swear."

I gave him a genuine smile. "Aw, come on. I have few pleasures in life. Intimidating folks is one of them. Besides, I don't want anyone thinking we're soft."

Silar snorted. "Trust me, no one thinks your soft. Now come on, let's go. This derelict gives me the creeps, and I want off of it five minutes ago."

I moved behind him as he joined the rest of his crew hauling the cargo from a hidden rig in the arena floor. "You were the one that picked the drop site. If you don't like it, why pick it?"

"I picked it because it's abandoned. I don't want to be here, which means no one else wants to be here, either. Fewer prying eyes, and all that. Sheesh, and here I thought you were the smart one of your crew."

I let that comment slide as I helped load the pallets and watched as the precious cargo was loaded onto the Lucky Duck.

My skin crawled as one crate passed me. It was

odd. A sweet taste seemed to enter my mouth though I smelled nothing out of the ordinary. Still, shudders rippled down my spine as if I was being watched. I looked around, knowing I would find nothing.

Silar went on alert. "What now?"

I shook my head as if trying to shake something off of me. "Nothing."

Silar narrowed his gaze at me. "I know it's not nothing. You have that look in your eye."

"What look?"

Praxis shrugged. "You know. That 'I'm going to kill something' look."

I lifted the corner of my mouth. "You seem to be an expert. Tell me, are you often in the receiving end of such a look?"

The male crossed his arms, his face flaming to a bright orange that nearly matched his hair. "As a matter of fact, yes. So tell me what's going down. I have a right to know. I don't want my crew being caught unawares." Then the color drained from Silar's face. "It's not mate trouble is it? You Rodinians and the whole mating thing--"

I raised my hand to stop what could have been a good rant. "You don't need to worry, Praxis. I'm unmated, and so far, fate has yet to reveal my mate to me." I ignored the pang twisting in my chest. Emotions—feelings—had no place out here. I'd already seen what had happened when the others stumbled upon their fate-mates while on mission.

I refused to let that happen to me.

But Silar was correct about something. There was a feeling in my gut that there was something amiss, and I hated that I couldn't put my finger on it. Ever since the tournament at the Concord of Sovereign Worlds, I had been on red alert, as if my whole body was itching for a fight.

"Just nerves, I guess. Maybe your talk about this place affected my perceptions." I only half believed what I said. "I'll grab my prowler and tuck in."

I commed the recruits, letting them know that everything was going as planned. They would follow behind us in slipstream. Once I fetched— then secured—my prowler onto the smuggler's ship, I paused again at the neatly secured cargo. One crate seemed to call to me.

"Reaper, are you coming?"

My head shot up and I peeked over the rim of the crate. Silar eyed me curiously. I forced myself away from the crate. I could be more cautious than the others on my team, but that was no without reason. There were lives at stake, and the last few months have proven that there was more happening beneath the surface than we had originally thought.

The fact that Legion command was essentially smuggling in supplies was proof of that.

I continued following Silar through the long halls of the Lucky Duck. The engine under us humming while the Lucky Duck moved through the derelict's exiting airways. "How long do you think it'll take?"

Silar smiled over his shoulder. "By tomorrow morning. Lunch time, the latest."

I raised an eyebrow. "Really?" We were deep in the Savage Lands Sector, the no man's land just outside of the Solarian Corridor. It would take a few days if not more to reach Legion command from here.

Silar shrugged. "I had some work done on the Lucky Duck. The whole space folding thing."

My ears perked up. Maybe he would drop some hints about his tech upgrades. "How did you get that?"

Silar pressed a finger to his lips. "It's a secret." He nodded toward a room on his left. "This is yours. Chow's in ten, if you're feeling peckish. Drop a comm if you need directions to the mess."

With that, the smuggler that made for an unlikely ally left me alone. I didn't quite trust the sparkle in his eye, and as I opened my accomodations, I realized why.

He had used one of his cargo hauls as my room. It was clear that he had come from a run from Terra Prime, as it was full of greenery and other foliage. Despite myself, I smiled. It had been a long time since I spent time planet-side, and especially long since I'd been anywhere with live plants. This was a treat, and I had Silar to thank for it.

I flopped down on a makeshift bed, leaning back against the pillows and raising comms to my lips. I paused, shaking my head at myself. Comms wouldn't work over this distance, but I would be able to send an encrypted wave through the nexus.

After entering a few access codes into my gauntlet, I spoke into the comms.

"Dorn to Aurum. Supplies have been acquired and secured. Now en route to Legion command. We'll be there in the approximately two days. The recruits are doing well, following in slipstream. New tech on the Lucky Duck. Will research more when there is a moment. Over and out." I sent the wave, and got ready for some down time.

I rested my head back against the pillows, gazing up at the dimly lit ceiling. My mind drifted to cargo bay. It was nothing I smelled before. It was wondrous and even now I was tempted to slip back into the loading dock and inhale my fill. I groaned and rubbed my head.

A nap would be good right about now. Commander Batair wanted me to train some recruits while I was at command. I rested my head on my arm and closed my eyes, inhaling deeply and imagining that smell. The darkness swallowed me and soon I was standing in a meadow filled with flowers.

Eva Priest writes otherworldly romances with strong heroines and the dominant alpha males who claim them.

amazon.com/author/evapriest

bookbub.com/profile/eva-priest

goodreads.com/evapriestwrites

facebook.com/evapriestwrites

instagram.com/evangelinepriest

twitter.com/evapriestwrites

Printed in Great Britain
by Amazon